The Raffle Baby

*An astounding lyrical novel inspired by a
shocking true story of the Great Depression.*

Ruth Talbot

Praise for The Raffle Baby

"This is one of those rare books where the reviewer wants to give it ten, no, a hundred, no, two thousand stars! The writing is stunning. Ruth Talbot has a delicate, beautiful usage of words."

— Trisha Sugarek, Reviewer

"Every word was music to my ears. So beautifully written I couldn't put it down."

— Amazon Reader

"I read books. I teach books. I have read only one other book among the thousands in my lifetime that moved me in this way. Any words that I could write to describe the haunting beauty of this tale would be, well, useless."

— Amazon Reader

"Once begun, I could not put this book down until I'd finished. Kudos to this author for a unique and emotionally satisfying story. The writing is poignant, witty and fresh. I can't recommend this book enough. Due to the intriguing title and premise, I went in with high expectations and they were more than rewarded. 5+ stars!"

— Goodreads Reader

"Finally! Something both very well-written and fresh! I loved every single page. Books like this one, although few and far between, are the reason I read."

— Amazon Reader

"The Raffle Baby lives up to its subtitle. The author succeeds in writing a beautiful, lyrical story."

— Goodreads Reader

"Great story telling and a mesmerizing writing style. It left me with tears in my eyes at the very end. An intriguing read for both the history and the fiction. By the time you made it through the first chapter you find yourself in the grip and rhythm of a unique writing style. This book just flows from then on. Loved it - worth ten stars!"

— Amazon Reader

"The author clearly knows the secrets of the human heart. More importantly, she knows how to translate those emotions into very moving words. Get ready for an emotional rollercoaster."

— Amazon Reader

"The Raffle Baby hits all the marks. A beautiful picture of this era of American history."

— Amazon Reader

For Jan and Bill Walker, who were there at the beginning. With all my love.

Author's Note

The story of the raffle baby is inspired by a 1933 article published in a North Carolina newspaper. Although the story was no more than two hundred words long, it captured my attention instantly, and held it for twenty years. I hope this story does the same for you.

Ruth Talbot, Minneapolis, January 2022

Chapter One

I must establish up front—to prevent any dashed hopes or misplaced anger—that I am not the raffle baby. Please do not be discouraged by this, for I promise you: fairytale, lullaby, soliloquy, myth. As you will discover, I am a man of precision. I will give you words. But only the ones you need. Hold out your hands. There. Now. Let's begin.

Most days I sit on the front porch of my cottage with my *Reader's Digest* and a cup of coffee, and whether it be day or night, I am now always in my own twilight. My eyesight is poor, but there is enough left that I can look into the past to tell you this tale. You are kind to listen to the ramblings of an old man.

See here. I have lived my potential, and I am content. I hope you can say that of your life. I worked my forty years and shored up my progeny so well that most are too busy to visit. I watched as my skin withered into translucence, like the papery wisps of an onion peel. But, is it not true that anything you can see through takes you someplace else?

In the solid middle years of my life Walter Mitty was my Lawrence of Arabia. Hear me now. This was by design and so it was good. Like you, perhaps, I have stood at the edge of an ocean, though it was too far away for me to touch. I plaited my love's hair on the day she died. And she kissed my hand and held it to her cheek, as if I had given her silks and spices from Atlantis.

I digress. But surely you will forgive an old man.

The story of the raffle baby begins with me in the Laurel Highlands of Pennsylvania. Trust me, I will get to her in time. But to know her, you must know me.

It was 1936, and the Great Depression gripped us like a circus strongman. Before, the men in my town descended deep into the coal mines, while the women kept house and tended children. The miners were a rowdy crew, until, all the veins exhausted, the miners of our town were forced to look for work elsewhere. Some left with promises to send money. Others, like my father, just up and walked away from everything, never to return.

The last we ever saw of him, Mother was running alongside his old truck, dirt and gravel flying up into her hair and face, her husband behind the wheel, moving faster than she thought that old, dilapidated truck could ever carry him. Ankles swollen with the moisture of a summer's humidity, it wasn't too long before the truck was gone and she was chasing a swirling cloud of dust that mixed with her breath and choked her from going on.

Was it unusual in those times for a mother to send her twelve-year-old son out into a world clogged with despair? No. There were plenty of us youngsters out there, riding the rails, stealing apples, hustling odd jobs. Tramps, they sometimes called us. But we were not ashamed. And I was fortunate. I was often hungry, but I did not starve. I might have been cold, but I did not freeze.

You might as well know that it was more than my mouth to feed that prompted my expulsion from our home. My father's void forced Mother into a place deep inside herself accessible only to her. I was grateful for the days when she looked at me but saw nothing. And I was frightened of her. Frightened of the uncharted geography of her temperament. Frightened of her many minefields and those grand sweeps of no-man's-land that bordered her every province, her every nation. After Father left, looking at my mother was like trying to read a map of an unknown land. Her face was a grid with lines pointing this way and that, her brow was a mountain range mired in self-pity. Her intentions were obscured by a harsh topography. I did not have the legend to traverse her, so I simply existed on the outskirts of her despair.

Even at twelve-years-old I understood how she had come to the precipice of an impossible choice. We lived in a tattered company house owned by the mine. With the mine shuttered, the families were told to move on. For a while, we lived in the small room above the butcher shop. Eventually our meager savings ran out, and so, I was sent away. After, I believe Mother kept house and cared for an elderly woman. But I cannot say for certain, as I never saw her again.

I roamed around the town for a few weeks, half praying Mother would change her mind, half hoping she would not. At night, I slipped through an unlocked window into the elementary school and curled up on the wrestling mats. I battled stray dogs for sustenance and drank and washed in the creek that threaded through an old mill.

It was in the five-and-dime on the main street that I saw the vast smallness of my life. In two minutes, I could walk, aisle-by-aisle, from one end of the store to the other, as if I were Louis and Clark exploring a new wilderness of motor oil, penny candy, cheap writing paper, and tobacco. I walked that mercantile terrain until I was finally ejected for soiling the comic books with my filthy fingers. The dirty hands and soiled shirt cuffs of a child were all people saw when they looked at me.

And so, I left the town, not just because I was hungry, but also because I hungered. I did not return for more than sixty years.

Yes. I know you are impatient to learn about the raffle baby. And I to tell you. I will jump ahead, just for you.

One evening, so very long ago, the girl with fiery red hair and too-big boots unraveled her tale to a ragged band of hoboes and migrant workers gathered around a spitting fire on a grower's farm in California. Our bellies were not full, but neither did they offer up their perverse pangs of hunger. It was warm, so we were not distracted by the cold that would inevitably return to invade our bones, unless we made it to Florida by October. By the end of the girl's story, I knew her audience did not believe her tale. And it makes no matter if I did or not.

But you. Perhaps you will find a seed of truth or a shard of lie playing hide-and-seek with my words. Perhaps not.

Come. My shadows are long. Be that I finish my story, and you stay with me to the end. For that is the only way you will know if she was my love. If I plaited her hair.

Chapter Two

Wwhat do twelve years prepare you for, when four are spent in the nursery and eight in short pants? A cat's eye marble is not the very earth on its axis, tilting you in the right direction. The tin soldier cannot protect. The toy car cannot whisk away.

But it did not matter, for I was lucky.

Think. Think of a time when you were lucky. A quarter under your shoe as you ambled along. A job that came out of nowhere. Curtains that never soil. A convertible acquired for a song because you reminded a dear old lady of a long-ago beau. It is sweet, is it not? Yes. Sweet like an apple cake I had yet to taste.

I was lucky because I was big for a twelve-year-old. I had reached five nine the previous year and this worked to my advantage. Can you see? Can you see the upper body strength it takes to swing yourself up onto a moving boxcar? Can you see the stamina required to walk ten miles on broken shoes until a kind farmer stops at your outstretched thumb?

I left my town on a mid-afternoon train headed north. Before Mother kicked me out, I had taken an old rucksack used to stop up a hole in the living room wall to keep out the rats. I stuffed it with clothes, my baseball and glove, three toy cars and an old wooden yo-yo my father made for my sixth birthday. I believe I brought these toys on my journey for comfort. Or perhaps it was because, despite my size, I was still a child and did not know better. But it was good that I did, for I could barter them for a ham sandwich and a glass of milk, a sack of apples, or some other necessity. And I was glad for it. You would have been, too.

As I entered the rail yard the sound of metal wheels screeching was surpassed only by that of a steam monster pouring into the sky. The sounds assaulted the soft places in my twelve-year-old consciousness. Nevertheless, as it slowed for a crossing, I ran down the tracks and hid behind tall grasses, then threw myself into an open boxcar when it passed, gripping my rucksack to my chest. I had not stopped to think what it would feel like to ride a boxcar. But I learned soon enough, for I felt every bump and splinter.

After an hour, the train slowed and curled into a curve as it chugged into the small city of Greensburg, where it stopped. From my perch, I watched hundreds of raggedy men jump from boxcars, emerging like one dark mass of humanity. They could have been a church congregation going to a revival, or the miners my father worked alongside preparing to descend into the earth for a shift. I felt this was as good a place as any to stop, so I jumped down and followed the ragtag band of tramps and hoboes.

I had never been outside my town, with its one main street and neat neighborhoods, so the bustling and jangling of people and commerce astounded me at first. But with each step I felt more confident, and I knew I would not turn back. Still, I was also cautious and hesitant. It is hard to explain, but you know what I mean. You have been there, each foot firmly planted at odds.

Those first days in the small city I quickly saw that I would have to use a third eye when I looked for what I needed. It was like this. Where once I saw a trash bin, I began to see an icebox. My fingers were the tines of a fork. My rucksack doubled as a pillow. An indentation under a bush, my bed. I collected crumpled newspapers to wrap under my socks to ease the shifting of my shoes that rubbed blisters into being. They were as good a band-aid as I had ever had. I learned that an eye that saw multiple uses for any one thing belonged to the boy who survived. I would be that boy.

There was the issue of cleanliness, and other personal ablutions you are wondering about. I did the best I could, like you did the best you could on a test you hadn't studied for, or a presentation you hadn't prepared for. I went to the bus station at the busiest hour, and lost in the crowd of travelers, I slipped into the men's room to wash and tidy. Just one more body, invisible in a throng. Outside the city, I washed and laundered in the streams and dried my clothes on the rocks. I gathered sturdy bark and scrubbed my teeth as best I could. I had read of this in a *Boy's Life* magazine and had laughed then at the notion of using a tree as a toothbrush. But it served me well until I could find alternate means.

All day I walked through the city streets, down into neighborhoods with houses that had not heard of the "Big Trouble." (You call this time the Great Depression; we knew it as the Big Trouble, for it was not depression that stung us, but trouble.) I watched other boys and men as they loitered, begged, and stole. But I could not bring myself to beg for food. I followed these shadowy figures on stealthy night journeys through trash bins in alleys. Once they had cleared from my sight, I followed suit, though I am sure I netted far less than they for my labors. But it kept me alive, did it not?

It was in one of those alleys, my head peering into a bin, that Vic found me, though I did not know his name then, of course. At first, I was frightened. He was bigger and taller than me. Well over six feet and sturdy. The sun was playing its early morning song just then, and as he came closer I saw smooth skin, not the wrinkles and slack-jaw jowls of the men I had seen stealing and hustling. His shock of yellow hair was a beacon in the soft light of dawn.

"You best move on," he said to me in a voice deep like the chimes of a grandfather clock. "Too close to dawn. Them bulls'll be coming 'round about now looking to roust us. You best get along out of sight with me."

I nodded mutely and followed him as he threaded through quiet city streets. Remember I told you I was lucky? Yes, indeed. I was lucky, and I followed him like a duckling follows its mother.

As we approached a parked bakery truck, engine still running, Vic stopped and directed me to crouch. We saw the driver hop down and hustle into a dimly lit diner with his delivery. As soon as he disappeared inside, Vic motioned us forward, and we ran to the back of the truck and I watched him grab at the still warm rolls and breads.

"Get a pie," he hissed, nodding at a neat stack of white boxes. I snatched one, then, as if I had done this all my life, another. And then we ran down the street. And another street. And another. Zig-zagging so I didn't know if we had a destination or were just running.

Vic told me to be quiet, but I laughed. Laughed because of the sheer exhilaration of thieving. Laughed because I would eat. I would eat one whole pie, I thought. Laughed because I was not alone.

Ours was an uncertain life in uncertain times, though, of course, there were a few certainties, all right. Some were sour, like unripe lemons on our tongues. Finding food and shelter was my constant occupation. And despite thousands of miles traveled over many years, survival would always be my destination.

But some certainties were good, at least for a while. Vic was one of them.

Now, this day, with you here with me, I can say my memories are my certainty. They have not gone anywhere. They wake me in the mornings and put me to bed at night. I have the certainty that I loved a girl all those years ago.

You have them too, in your world. Your guarantees. Your certainties. And they carry you through your life. What comfort certainty brings! What are yours? A stainless-steel fridge that always hums for you. The neighborhood pool that opens every Memorial Day. Your three-car garage that plays the music of a violin trio when you hit the remote and a door rumbles open. Are you surprised that an old man of ninety some years, who sits on a porch, knows such things? Here I laugh, for my granddaughter and great-grandchildren find comfort in these same circumstances. The rhythm of certainty provides the comfort of predictability.

Now see here. We were not bums or tramps. We were hoboes who worked and had coins in our pockets. A dime would fetch a hot meal. Fifty cents a shower and a bed for the night. The tramps worked if they wanted. The bums did nothing until they found themselves on a chain gang. But oh, how we worked. We stretched and struggled for pay that laughed in our faces and did not cover our feet. We were grateful when a farmer gave us a dollar a day and a barn to sleep in. We followed the seasons, chasing them like we chased the trains. We harvested hay in Nebraska and Iowa and picked peas in Oregon. Strawberries in Colorado. We ate the bruised castaways by the dozens, until we were sick in the hedges. You can imagine, can't you? I will never eat a strawberry again. There was cotton down Texas way, but we'd rather beg our way through the cold than do that thankless work.

But that is yet to come. I am getting ahead of myself.

After our pre-dawn bakery raid, I followed Vic along the tracks, though I did not know where we were headed. It did not matter. We had stuffed the rolls and one pie in my rucksack. As we walked, we ate the bread, so rich with the pungent, welcome taste of yeast. Then Vic beckoned for the pie box I carried, and we sat by the roadside, passing it between us, digging through the crust and sticky apple filling like toddlers. We passed a small rail yard where desperate men ran frantically from men armed with rifles. I watched as they scattered. There were too many desperate souls for the train police to catch. More than three-quarters escaped onto the train, which grew smaller as it chugged away. The men raised their hands to us and hooted from the boxcar doors as they passed.

Vic pointed up to a rocky incline to where a slum hung by the proverbial thread. We were never to beg or pull a job in the slums. They were as poor as we.

He told me a little of himself as we walked. He was fifteen and had been on the road for three years. He had lived with a foster family that had thrown him out after they lost their savings, their car, and finally their home.

"But that was just fine by me," he said, his words as deliberate as they were sparse. "The man had taken a strap to me one too many times and I was glad to go."

He did not ask me of myself, neither did he ever tell me why he had taken me under his protection. But somehow, I knew it was because someone must have done the same for him. Or not—and he had suffered as a result. There was humanity on those roads and rails. And the kind of evil you never forget.

We walked along dusty rail tracks. The trains rumbled their parallel course, and we would step back to watch as they passed, men clinging to the catwalks, others resting on top, leaning on their elbows, some visible in the open boxcars. We raised a hand to those who saw us from their perches, sitting together like birds on a wire.

As we walked, Vic explained the way of the hoboes. I was never again to travel alone. Or fall asleep atop a boxcar in daylight. The hot summer sun could burn blisters onto my face if I was careless. It was not good to ride a hotshot train if I was starving or even just weak with hunger, for it made fewer stops, which meant fewer places to find work or hustle a meal. But if I was in a hurry, well that was fine, then, wasn't it? If I rode atop a train, which Vic was not inclined to do, I was to tie myself down. I could nap then, in the curl of cool days, without fear of falling overboard. Then he told me the story of a poor soul he had pulled from the track once a train had run over him when he slipped from the catwalk. He had lost both arms, and the good Lord had not seen fit to let him die. There are other such stories that I could tell you. But if you heard them, you would not be the same. I will spare you the sound of what I saw all those years ago.

Hitting the stem meant going into town to beg. Stealing was permitted, but we were not to be greedy. Vic's eyes lingered on mine as he spoke, and I knew he was referring to the second pilfered pie.

I was to remember safe places and people who were kind and generous, for we would need to return to them. He produced a worn *Reader's Digest* from his rucksack. It had been bent in half, like the first crease in folding a piece of paper into a toy airplane. He handed me the worn magazine, and I flipped through the pages of small meticulous writing crowding the margins. He had written the names of towns and people. Drawn tiny maps. Applied symbols to each. I read words and phrases I had not heard before.

Every life has its own language. Those first weeks, I stuttered through the new words of the road, forcing my mouth to carry this unfamiliar vocabulary. A reefer was a refrigerator car. If you got locked in one of those you might freeze to death. The bundle a man carried at the end of a stick bouncing on his shoulder made him a bindle stiff. And you never got too close to another's belongings, or let them get too close to yours, lest they slit your throat for a pair of boots.

Spoken slang and written symbols were my ABCs and 123s. I also learned the nomenclature of friend and foe. There were bulls, wolves, and buzzards on the rails. An animal kingdom where I was the prey.

Perhaps an aside is needed here as you may be wondering, who were those predators? The plain-clothed train detectives and sheriff's deputies, known for their bullying and brutality, and called bulls, prowled the rail yards and met arriving trains with bullets and crowbars, trying to get at the 'boes who jumped before the station. They rounded up the 'boes who would sometimes overrun a town already burdened with transients. They took them to jail or marched them to the county line and forced them across to become someone else's problem. Sometimes they just shot a man on the spot for not moving fast enough. The wolves and buzzards. Well, they liked younger, innocent boys like me, and plied us with food, socks, and candy. You can see, in your mind, what came next.

Unless you were lucky.

Chapter Three

By the time Vic and I stopped traveling that first day together, the bread had long fulfilled its purpose, and dusk accompanied us for the last hour of our march. Finally, we detoured and scrambled up a rise and past a stream where we crawled through a thicket, then emerged into a clearing and a jungle. I had heard of these jungles, of course, and seen one from a distance, but had been too afraid to venture in. A jungle, despite its misleading name, was a safe haven for 'boes. Some were small and temporary. Later I would see larger jungles in big cities, ringed with shacks and other crude dwellings made of cardboard, tin, and fruit crates.

As I emerged from the bushes, I saw a dozen men lounging about, some staring into nothing, another repairing a shoe, another sewing a patch to his pants. There was a grace to the gathering, as if rules had descended upon the space, just as rules kept order in a classroom. This place had the potential to be a cesspool, and those who didn't live on the fringe probably thought this was so. But they tried, these 'boes, and this showed in a shirt that was as white as it could be, a shaving mirror nailed to a tree, bedrolls tucked neatly away when not in use.

But they were raggedy despite their efforts. I did not know it then, but I was seeing myself reflected in their faces. Their clothes were dirty and torn. One man was so thin he had wrapped a rope through his belt loops three times to hold up his pants. I stared in sinking fascination at a face obscured by soot. I would later discover, by hard experience, that this was the result of riding a coal car located directly behind the engine.

A man in a tatty brown suit and porkpie hat pulled low over his ears stood over a pot and stirred something that smelled like home.

They all looked up when they heard us. The man stirring the pot with a stick nodded at Vic.

"It's the Viking!" he exclaimed. "Come back to call. What say you Vic?"

Vic nodded back. "We're swell, Georgia Joe. You're looking aces, but that shirt needs a good wash."

The man laughed, and it was comforting to see the spirit of recognition and acceptance.

We dropped our bags and sat around the fire, though I was uncomfortable in my uncertainty. I looked to Vic as my compass. We produced the rolls and second pie and were greeted with applause. Then the stew was doled out. Another 'bo came in soon after us and emptied tins of lima beans and corn into the pot, then sat next to Vic. Each man produced a bowl. Some were tin. Others carved from wood or gourds. The rolls were divided, then divided again, and passed around. Georgia Joe sliced the pie into slivers to be enjoyed later. I watched the rusty knife do its bidding, ashamed of my distress as the whole disappeared into smaller and smaller parts that would have to be shared.

The men ate heartily, laughing and joking as only men who have shared misery can. It was a while until they noticed I was not eating. A tramp called Bo Wrinkles, who wore his name on his face, produced a tin cup from his bundle. He held it out to me and I grabbed for it, but he snatched it away and hugged it to his bony chest, sunken under sparse and wiry silver hairs. I looked around and saw a shirt hanging in a tree above him.

"He means to trade," said another 'bo, who wore a blue bandanna on his head and one tied around his neck. He was named Blue, I would learn, and he was seventeen. Just another man-child in an army of boys and girls who had run away because the road was better than home.

In a quicksilver knowing, I understood that given names were of no use in the jungle. We were identified by some feature or quirk and then christened with a moniker. Georgia Joe was from Atlanta. Vic was short for Viking. I was soon to receive mine. Yes, you want to know what it is, but you must wait. For it is a story in itself.

Blue stretched out his leg and kicked my rucksack. "Show us what you got."

I looked to Vic for reassurance. He nodded.

I studied the old man, wondering what I had that could possibly meet his needs. In the end, I pulled out the baseball, one toy car, and the yo-yo. Bo Wrinkles took a long moment to study the items. So long in fact that the others lost interest and resumed their talking. Finally, the old man snatched the yo-yo and threw the tin mug at me. Promptly someone served me stew, which was so thick I could eat it with my fingers, mopping up the dregs with my piece of roll. I watched Bo Wrinkles wind out the string, then fold it bit over bit and tie it into a knot. He deposited it and the wooden wheel into the depths of his pack. After finishing his stew, he was soon snoring like a man who owned a pressed suit and shiny shoes.

All 'boes were welcome in the jungle, as long as they contributed to the pot or could supply firewood or such. We could stay a night or a few days or longer, catching our breath, regaining our strength. But we always had to contribute something. Some snared rabbits and squirrels, others brought pilfered vegetables.

Someone might bring a bar of soap and sandwiches acquired from a kindly farm wife.

But, it was different with her. Now you must pay attention here, as this is when she enters the story, full onto the stage like Juliet.

She came that evening, the first I spent with Vic in the jungle, emerging just as we had, out of the thicket. Now, most girls on the road cut their hair and dressed like boys. It was safer to be disguised and travel in groups. But not her. She wore a pleated dark green skirt, a stretched-out blue sweater and black lace-up men's boots that were too big. Her hair was flame red and it cascaded past her shoulders. I didn't see then, but would when she sat with us, that her hands were clean, and her nails painted the red of candied apples and fire engines. But what I noticed most about her was how small she was. Barely five feet and thin like a reed. Later, when I saw her next to Vic, I could only laugh. If she sat on his knee they could have done a traveling ventriloquist show.

The same man who greeted us, Georgia Joe, welcomed her with a reverence a father might use for a daughter, and motioned for her to sit.

She sunk neatly onto a large flat rock, and primly tucked her legs underneath her. She opened her rucksack, which looked like it had once belonged to a soldier, and produced a tin plate and an army knife that folded out a spoon and two blades. She put these in front of her and looked at us.

We all stared back. I don't think any of us had seen a creature quite like her in some time, if ever.

It was Blue who broke the silence, reminding her that a 'bo only ate if he contributed to the pot. The others nodded and hmm-hmmed in agreement. All I could do was stare. She looked like a porcelain doll I had seen in a shop window in Greensburg just a few days earlier. What does one do with such a doll, but love it?

She looked around the circle of men before her, like a queen might survey her subjects. The rock she had selected was high enough that she looked down upon us.

"I have something better," she told us, steady as that rock under her. "I have a story."

Without hesitation, Georgia Joe motioned for her to pass her plate. He filled it and passed it back. She set it on the rock beside her, and began to speak, stirring a magic we hadn't known was inside us. When she spoke of mountains, it was as if she had known them as infants. When she described a stream, she was the first drop of water to fall upon the rocks.

Chapter Four

I must tell you of her voice. Some voices sound like a door closing, others like a downy chick peeping. Her voice was like none I had heard before. It bore a sweet, sing-songy drawl, and she stretched some words out so far, they might as well have turned a corner.

She was a gypsy girl, she told us, and was running away to Tennessee to meet a gypsy prince who was forbidden to marry her. She was to go to Grandfather Mountain in the town of Elk Grove. He would come for her under the outcropping of rocks that resembled the profile of an old man.

Then she started her proffered story.

"When I was eleven-years-old, my ma sold me to a woman leading a gypsy caravan. They were outcasts, like us, and preferred to travel their long distances on donkey trails that curled through forests, where they were less likely to be seen. They preferred the very isolation that was slowly killing Ma and me.

"They came once a year to our little cabin in the hills, arriving almost to the day. My ma welcomed them, thinking if she was nice to them, they would be nice to us. She allowed them to park their brightly colored caravans in the wood by the stream, next to our cabin, and let their horses feed in the grasses beyond.

"Now, my father was gone by this point. Died of a fever when I was three. I had almost died, too. When it was just me and Ma, she fed us on squirrels, rabbits, vegetables, and the wild roots and greens she foraged in the woods. We had no cow for milk or butter, and only a few scraggly chickens gave us eggs. And the land. All those woods. Well, they weren't really ours. If we had owned property, don't you think we would have sold and moved to town and bought ribbons for our hair?

"We had no sugar or coffee until the gypsies came. In exchange for our hospitality, they shared their bounty, and we ate like kings in their company. My ma cried when they moved on. She liked their carefree ways, their full larders, and silver bracelets. We had no such things. When they left, they took the sounds of the hills with them. And all was quiet again.

"They always came around my birthday when the greening had spread across the mountain. We would hear them a mile away, their horses grunting, their caravan wheels thumping, their singing like staccato birdsong. I would skip through the woods to meet them, giddy with the first glimpse of red, blues, and golds flashing through the green of the trees.

"The winter before I turned eleven had been a hard one, for we had not foraged and stored enough. We went days without food until one of our traps took. We were saggy sacks of bones. The old gypsy woman, who was always at the reins of the lead caravan, noticed immediately. None of them spoke much English, but we all understood the voice of starvation.

"They settled their horses and then immediately brought out dried meats and canned tomatoes and corn. My ma drank from a bottle.

"The old lady built a fire. She wore a red swirl skirt and black brocade jacket. Her thin silver bracelets snaked up her arm and tinkled as she mixed flour, spices and water, and fried bread in a skillet. After, there were sweet, dried figs. We ate this way for a week.

"Later, the old gypsy woman told me that my ma said she had never seen me happier than with breadcrumbs in my lap and sticky honey smeared across my face.

"I believe it was a hasty transaction born of desperation rather than reason. Later I learned that one of the young gypsy men took a knife to the old lady's hem, and gold coins fell out. These were pressed into Ma's hands. She patted my head and told me to be a good girl. Then another gypsy man hoisted me up and before I knew it I was in the caravan and it was moving. While I was gorging myself I hadn't noticed that the gypsies had packed their belongings and hitched up the horses."

When the girl paused to take a few bites of stew, we peppered her with questions and suspicions.

Georgia Joe, who had seniority in the jungle, went first. "Why would a gypsy family take on a little girl in hard times?"

Bo Wrinkles, who had awoken at some point, chimed in. "Why do you think, you stupid boy."

"Oh, you old pervert, go back to sleep," Georgia Joe commanded.

That exchange finished, we looked back at the girl.

"Why, they took me to dance, of course. The old gypsy woman, whose name was Magda, taught me how to dance so my blouse slid off one shoulder just so, and my skirt, when lifted ever so slightly, revealed a bare calf. When I danced, I wore her silver bracelets and a scarf so purple you might mistake it for grapes if you were starving.

"I danced in the town squares until we were chased away. I danced in the slums while Magda told fortunes to desperate souls, and her sons, Markos and Milos, collected pennies and dimes. In summertime, we might travel with a circus or carnival. We roamed the South, and sometimes ventured north as far as Maine where we picked blueberries. And this is how we lived for years. They were perfectly nice to me and I did not miss my ma for I ate every day and slept in Magda's brightly colored caravan, tucked away in a trundle bed. The inside walls were lined with quilts and beads, and I fell asleep to the gentle swaying of passing days."

"Say something in gypsy," Blue commanded.

"Where are your gypsy clothes?" a 'bo named Mule asked.

"Gypsy is not a language," she answered, as if speaking to a small child. "And they did not teach me their language, I taught them mine. They got along better after that, being able to trade and conduct themselves in English."

She polished off her stew and Georgia Joe passed her a sliver of pie.

"So why did you leave if life was so good?" I asked.

"She already told us that, stupid," Blue said. "She left to marry the gypsy prince."

"Ain't no such thing," Bo Wrinkles said.

The girl ignored us and continued.

"It is a little more complicated than that. As I grew older, my fair complexion and fine bones made me look more and more like a waif in a storybook. Magda and her sons were large-boned, solid people. Their eyes, skin, and hair were as dark as the very earth. When others looked at us they grew suspicious, for gypsies were known to snatch or buy babies. I became aware, a year ago, that Magda meant to marry me off. I was grown and it was time to close the circle my mother had started. I wasn't sure how long until I became someone's bride, but I prepared myself for escape if I was not happy with Magda's choice. I sneaked coins and sewed them into the hem of my gypsy skirts. I put dried meats and nuts in my drawstring bag."

"If you're so rich, girly, then give us your coin instead of this stupid story," Bo Wrinkles groaned.

We shushed him. There was plenty of time to get to the subject of money.

"Every year, gypsies come together down West Virginia way to swap stories, trade goods, and settle bets. It was here I met Alfonso, the gypsy prince. He was so handsome that all the girls put sweet honey on their lips and rose water behind their ears. Ten families gathered just a few months ago. There was dancing and drink. Oh, you've never seen so much color until you see the gypsies twirling and stomping.

"And, of course, there were betrothals and weddings, often in the same week. I looked over the other young men who had arrived. Did Magda mean to marry me to one of them?

"Alfonso was required to marry a pure-blooded gypsy girl. But you see, he loved me. Because we were forbidden to marry, we ran away. We went separately, of course, so no one would be suspicious.

"And that is why I am here."

She had run through woods and mountains and walked the by-ways, she told us. She had survived by foraging for persimmons and wild asparagus and picking mushrooms and berries. She could do the same for us, she told no one in particular, as she planned to reunite with a small band of gypsies who would weave ribbons into her hair to make her presentable again to meet her prince.

Blue and Georgia Joe asked her question after question. Later, as I lay under the stars, I took out her answers and examined them one by one.

Her gypsy clothing had been stolen the day before by two farm girls who coveted them. They waited until she was bathing in a stream and they ran away with her swirling red skirt, peasant blouse, black stockings, and even her orange velvet shoes. In their place, they left behind the old green skirt and blue sweater. And when her clothes were lost, so was her modest fortune, for it had been sewn into the hem of her skirt.

She had ended up here—when she meant to travel to Tennessee—because she was hitchhiking and didn't know she was headed in the wrong direction.

I did not believe that she was running away to meet her gypsy prince. But, say, upon reflection, what better place to look for a shadowy monarch than in a jungle with a buzzard and a troupe of runaway vagabonds?

If her story was a stone in her pocket, it would be covered with grit and have nowhere to go.

I awoke the next morning to the rustling sounds of men and boys ducking out of the jungle to relieve themselves. As Vic and I readied to leave, the girl rolled her blanket into her rucksack and heaved the pack onto her shoulders. She still wore the old leather boots that clearly were too big. But they were sturdy and well-polished.

She caught me staring at them.

"They look worse than they are," she said. "I have newspaper stuffed down into the toes. I get by."

As Vic and I said our farewells and started walking, she followed, as if it were the most natural thing in the world. I think she believed that she would forage food for us and cook us greens and mushrooms in the next jungle. I know now that we were the gypsy princes she needed.

Since it was May, Vic said we would head to Iowa for the first cutting of the hay harvest. I looked at him doubtfully, having never held a pitchfork, much less lifted one. We both looked at the girl, silently telling each other that we were certain she had never even seen a pitchfork.

We followed the river and tracks for miles, then we stopped after the rail yard and crouched in tall grasses that bordered the tracks. All around us men and boys waited. We were one eye, one ear. We heard the Pennsylvania and Ohio freight, headed west, start up on the tracks and rumble. The whistle blew and the lights blinked. It starts slow, you see. Slow enough that a man can grab a catwalk ladder or jump up into a boxcar.

"Now!" Vic yelled.

I ran. Everyone ran, as if propelled by the starting gun at the Kentucky Derby. The chaos consumed me, and I felt the pull of the crowd. The train chugged toward us, gaining momentum. Vic jogged twenty feet ahead of me, grabbed the catwalk, and hung on for purchase. Once he had achieved his balance, he would climb atop the car. We were to meet in the middle and would have to keep our balance while picking our way through the dozens of 'boes that had already staked their claims.

I meant to grab the next ladder I could. I knew if I hesitated I could slip below the train and lose a leg. Or worse. When I was ready I reached out for the catwalk and scrambled with my feet to find a rung. My right hand slipped and I nearly went flying off, but the train traveled slowly enough that I could right myself and scramble aboard.

When we were both atop and headed toward each other, Vic started shaking his head.

"Dammit. Where's that frill?"

I looked behind us, not knowing what a "frill" was. But I saw that the girl wasn't there.

"Shit," Vic said, one of the few times I would ever hear him swear. "I reckon we ought to go back and get her."

I didn't move, surprised by his generous suggestion, though I agreed with it.

"We can't leave her out there on her own," Vic said. "It's not safe in the jungles for a girl alone."

He hopped down first, then I. Here's what you need to know about hopping off. It's just as dangerous as onboarding. Why? Because if you don't hit the ground running, you're going to break a leg. Or two. Luckily, the train was still chugging slowly on the track.

"It's that skirt," Vic said. "I shoulda thoughta that. Can't jump a train in no skirt."

We walked on and then I asked, "Do you think there really is a gypsy prince?"

"Well, sure, just not one waiting for her at whatever mountain. She just fed us a load of baloney for her meal."

"Yeah," I agreed, "but wasn't it nice, just for a little while, to think of something other than your belly?"

Vic answered with the dirt his shoe kicked up.

She appeared on the horizon then, as a tiny speck. As we grew closer the wind whipped her hair and her skirt flapped at us.

We stopped, facing each other, boxers in a ring about to bust some trouble.

"Well, boys," she finally said. "Took you long enough."

"Now, see here," Vic said, "we didn't have to come back for you. Why didn't you say you'd never jumped a train before?"

"Well, you didn't ask, now did you?"

"C'mon," Vic commanded, and started walking away from the tracks.

"Where to?" I asked, secretly glad we weren't going to jump another train just then.

"Pittsburgh. Gonna get some clothes for this girl so she can ride with us. Then we're going to have a lesson in riding the rails. And then, we're going to find us a meal and get outta here."

The girl's rucksack banged against her back and her boots clomped.

"Guess she'll need some shoes, too," I suggested.

"Guess so," Vic agreed.

We walked along the tracks, watching hundreds of men, like pills on an old sweater, lounge on the top of passing cars. That would be us soon enough.

Chapter Five

When we entered the buzz and brick of downtown, we followed Vic as you might follow a guide in a museum. I saw things I had never seen before. A line of men stretched like a coil of smoke for three blocks. Youngsters just like us stood on street corners, caps in hand. Other men just sat on the sidewalk, backs against the storefronts, not looking at anything. All were tattered and worn around the edges. They were like tiny ants at a picnic, I thought, not enough of a nuisance to really bother with, but enough trouble that you don't want them around. I watched better dressed people walk by this inhumanity, diverting their gazes.

I looked down at my own clothes. Just two weeks on the road and they were already grimy from using my shirt as a napkin and sleeping on the ground. But compared to the clusters of men and boys, my pants and blue work shirt looked like I had just walked out of the small department store back home sporting a brand-new going-to-church suit. I gaped at the filthy plaid and striped poverty around me.

Have you ever tasted your town? Silly notion, I know. You can't taste a town, unless you're an Okie, then you taste red clay earth, and your children taste only starvation. But when I was on that downtown street I tasted it, and it tasted like glass shards.

Vic pulled me out of the street just before a wagon mowed me down. He grabbed at the girl, too, and before I could say boo, he tore her skirt and was working on her sweater.

"Hey," she yelled, flapping at him with her hands to get him away. "Whadya do that for? I don't have any other clothes."

"Exactly," Vic said.

He grabbed a handful of dirt from the ground and ground it into her hair and onto her face. She was so surprised she didn't say anything. And no one around us seemed the least bit interested. Just a bunch of dirty 'boes proving everyone right with their dirty doings.

Then Vic gave instructions. She was to walk along the street in her torn clothes, asking for change. He gave her his cap. She was to drag her leg a bit, like she was lame.

"Don't make eye contact," he said. "And be sure you say, 'yes ma'am.' Don't stop in front of a man or a couple. Only approach a woman alone. If you see a woman in a car, you can ask her, too. Don't ask for a quarter. Ask for a penny and you'll get a dime."

She was shaking her head.

"But you can't leave me," she squawked. "What if something happens to me?"

Vic laughed, something I hadn't yet heard. "Well, you made it all the way from West Virginia on your own. I figure you can make it on a city street in broad daylight without much trouble."

She scowled and narrowed her eyes. "But why can't you stay?"

"We can't stay," Vic explained patiently, "because if you're a girl alone folks'll more than likely give you a little something."

She asked, "But what are you going to do?"

"We're gonna find you some clothes and then we're coming back for you," Vic said, patience wearing thin.

We left then. I looked back to see the girl still standing on the corner, Vic's hat in hand. I gave her an encouraging smile and a hand motion that I hoped said, "Go on now, it'll be fine."

Despite all her bravado, she looked like a helpless waif just then. She had told us that she was nineteen, but I didn't believe her. She was fifteen if she was a day.

My belly reminded me that I hadn't eaten since the night before, and I hoped we might pick up some bread along with the clothes, but Vic didn't say one way or another when or where we would eat.

He whistled some, with his hands in his pocket. Without the cap, his bright yellow hair looked like a dandelion. He had the golden complexion of a Norseman, which I had read about in a schoolbook. To me, he looked like the Viking Georgia Joe had seen. But I knew when others saw him all they perceived was a dirty bum. They never looked closely enough to see the difference between a bum and a 'bo. Vic was fifteen, but because of his size, he looked like a giant dirty bum. And so, I understood that he needed us as much as we needed him. People would be more sympathetic to a slip of a girl than they would to a towering, dirty Viking with tufts of fly-away yellow hair.

We walked into an alley, past the back doors that led to a barbershop, greengrocer, charity shop and newsstand, then we turned back onto the street and stopped in front of the charity store.

"This is where I need you to listen," Vic said.

I nodded.

And then he told me how we would get the clothes for the girl. He would walk into the store and look around. There were always good clothes up front and the clerk would be on him like white on rice, figuring he was there to steal something. While the clerk gave him the evil eye, I would wait in the back alley, and run in and grab trousers, a shirt, and if I could, shoes. I must try my hardest to find something that would fit the girl. If there were customers, I was to wait outside until they left.

My heart started beating faster. It was like the bakery truck all over again, but this time I already knew it would be exhilarating. I had felt the power of a stolen pie.

Vic spit into his hands, patted down his hair and tucked his ratty shirt into his pants. He was trying to look presentable, but it had little effect. His white shirt was the color of weak tea and his pants bore patches on each knee.

"Let's go," he commanded.

I doubled back and waited by the open back door of the charity shop. I stood surrounded by trash bins and old milk crates. Someone had dumped an ashtray right outside the door. The door to the shop was grimy with greasy streaks and fingerprints around the handle. Were those left by other people like me? Thieves and beggars? Tramps and 'boes?

I darted into the back of the shop and hid behind a pile of clothes and broken furniture. I crab walked a little closer to the curtain that separated the back room from the sales floor and peeked through to see Vic looking at a suit on a rack near the front window. Sure enough, a little man stood next to him, his back to me. His grey suit was shiny and he had black hair slicked so thoroughly that a penny on its edge would stick to the crown of his head. That's all I needed to see. I scurried to a pile of clothes and pawed through it like a dog unearthing a bone. I remembered what Vic had said about not being greedy and chose a pair of sturdy canvas pants and two work shirts that looked on the small size. They would still be too big for the girl, but I had done my best. I snatched up a belt. I heard the man coming back, and I had to leave without shoes. I ran until I thought my lungs would explode.

Vic stopped me the next block over.

"Don't run," he said. "If you run they know you done something wrong."

I skidded to a slow walk and he examined my finds as we walked back to where we had left the girl.

"You did good, sonny. Real good."

I basked in his praise. It was like jam on bread. And from then on I was known as Sonny Boy.

I had expected to see an angry girl on the corner, but instead, she was triumphant.

She held out the cap and Vic counted out eighty cents while she squealed and hugged me, then kissed me right on the cheek. She jumped and hopped and clapped her hands.

Vic grabbed her by her wrist to stop her and hissed, "You're supposed to be lame, remember?"

Adequately shamed, she stopped her celebrating. I saw her spirit collapse into itself momentarily, then reappear so quickly I wasn't sure I had really seen it slip away.

She grabbed my arm and threaded her hand through it. We walked slowly and she dutifully continued her pretend limp. It didn't matter to me that she was using me as a buffer against Vic's harshness.

Are you a middle child? Black sheep? Over achiever? Think of your familial place. How do you fit?

In our fledgling family, Vic was the disciplinarian and planner. He always knew which direction was north. I was the obedient child. I did all that was asked of me without question or complaint. The girl was the rebellious, unpredictable teenager. She exasperated Vic, but I worshiped her.

And now, today, if you were here with me on this porch, you would see that my shirt and pants are pressed to soldier-worthy creases. My boots are shined. My sheepdog, at my feet, is properly licensed and vaccinated. I never outgrew the obedience Vic drilled into me on the road.

That first day the three of us were together, we took the girl's earnings to a diner, which was just about as dirty as we were. We had to walk past a line of scraggly men begging for scraps. Do you think that was hard? Of course, it was. Some things I don't have to tell you.

We took turns washing in the bathroom, and the girl transformed herself with the clothes we had acquired for her.

For a dime each we got fried eggs, toast, hash browns, and even a slice of bacon. And the waitress refilled our coffee mugs three times even though a sign next to the cash register said no free refills.

When we were done, the waitress brought us each a piece of apple cake and winked at us conspiratorially.

"The old man just stepped out for a smoke. This is on me, kids."

As we ate our cake and talked, Vic included the girl in our plans as if it was a foregone conclusion that she would be with us, not just for that day, but when we harvested hay in Iowa, picked strawberries in Colorado, and apples in Washington. And she did not object, which made me realize there was no gypsy prince. No Grandfather Mountain.

I daren't ask her to tell us about herself. I thought it best that we play along and pretend we believed her story. How could I ask for something she had already given us?

"Do they have dollhouses in the gypsy caravans?" Vic asked, once he declared we would catch a freight leaving that night and head toward Iowa as planned.

"Why do you want to know?" she asked, smiling. She liked it when we posed questions. I could tell from the way she shifted her torso, pointing one shoulder toward us.

"Because you're so teeny you could just about live in a dollhouse. With a teeny tiny dog and a teeny tiny bed."

Can I tell you how nice it was to laugh, and to have my laughter flow into theirs? We were together, now, the three of us, and do you know this eased the road? It made the jungle stew taste better and helped me find thread to fix the tears in our clothes.

Vic sealed the unspoken arrangement when he asked, "What's your name, girly? If we're going to be traveling companions you might as well tell us."

Yes, I know, you want to know her name. But on the road, with your pitiful belongings on your back, what else did you have but your name? And you used it sparingly. I never did learn Vic's real name. Or hers.

She did not speak for so long that I thought she hadn't heard the question. Finally she said, "Teeny is just fine."

Vic shrugged and we finished our cake in silence. From then on, we were Vic, Sonny Boy and Teeny.

The cake had been our wafer. The third cup of coffee our wine.

Chapter Six

After that delicious meal, we jumped trains until we reached Iowa. Oh, so many ways to ride. The daredevils rode on the couplers between cars. I was convinced that those who rode the little shelf under the cars had a death wish. Finding an empty boxcar was sweet, like a candied red cherry on a long-ago-tasted sundae.

Vic knew the schedules and signals, and after enough time with him, we would come to learn them, too. And Teeny did learn to ride the rails. I think being so small and nimble made it easier for her to pull herself up the catwalk. And many were the times when she caught a train and we didn't. She'd hop off, double back to find us and tease us mercilessly.

Do you want to hear the words of road and rail? Maybe better you should experience them for yourself. Go. Go to the grimiest, dirtiest part of your town. Roll in the street until you are covered in dust. Walk through the city dump until someone holds their nose when you walk past. Then find a neon sign and stand two inches away and just watch it blink and blink until you are almost blind. Oh, but you are not done yet. You must trip and fall in the dirt and scrape your knees and elbows until you draw blood. And then you must get up and do it all again and again and again. Even this would not prepare you for the chaos of the rails.

We spent those first months together helping an Iowa farmer harvest his hay. Grand sweeps of grasses swayed in greeting. In these fields, Vic and I did the work of men and received half the wages. Teeny was taken into the house to help the farm wife with daily chores. Vic and I slept in the barn. Teeny slept on a thin mattress on the screened-in porch. Her hands were as red and chapped from lye as ours were calloused. That's when I realized she worked as hard as we did.

The farmer's daughter, heavy in her seventh month, slowed her mother down, and Teeny told us this was the subject of many a conversation in the evenings. In the end, it was decided that when the harvest was over, we would leave, and Teeny would stay to help finish the canning and do the farm chores the pregnant daughter could no longer do. There was no more work for us, and we would say our goodbyes in August, with promises to come back in six weeks to collect her.

On our last night together, the farmer allowed the three of us to sit on the front porch swing. From the kitchen window, his wife kept eyes on us, her face as sour as the lemonade her husband had instructed her to serve us. No doubt she had left the sugar out on her own accord. But it was no matter, for we were flush with cash. Fifty cents a day each for backbreaking work. But it was rewarding to see the bales, stacked together in self-satisfaction. If we could have got a penny for every pitchfork full of hay we pitched up on that wagon we would have been rich. Vic kept the money in a leather wallet deep inside his jacket.

Teeny had not told any more stories since we had been together. After our evening meals we all dropped onto our respective pallets and slept, too exhausted for talk, but content with our growing pockets.

"What will you do?" she wanted to know.

"Six weeks is a long time," Vic observed. "There's time to go to Colorado and pick strawberries."

We would need to save as much cash as possible for winter when there were just as many 'boes and far fewer jobs. We might need to rent a room here and there. The missions wouldn't keep kids more than a night, and girls were marched to the closest sheriff's office or police station to be sent home. We would also try our luck with the citrus harvest in southern Florida.

We said our good-byes like men: shaking hands and pressing the toes of our shoes in the dirt.

We left Teeny pulling weeds in the flowerbeds in front of the house. The daughter, who seemed to grow larger each minute, sat in the shade of the porch, her swollen feet propped in front of her. Sometimes she hollered at Teeny to hurry up and fetch her a glass of water. If this bothered Teeny, she never said. We had taught her to hold her pleases and ma'am's and thank you's in her hand, always at the ready to dole out. She knew the importance of a clean front. And it was she who was always telling us to wash our hands and clean our clothes regularly.

Look. Look at your own cuffs. We rolled our cuffs under to hide the grime but still we wore the road on our backs, and it was no use. But we tried, to please Teeny.

Those weeks without her, we followed dirt roads through one town and another, hitching some, and walking when the weather was fine.

It's funny to say but without Teeny we could be . . . boys. We did the things that boys do, but don't do in front of girls. You know what I mean. Do you really need me to go into detail?

Without Teeny we could walk longer and faster. There were long stretches of merciful silence without her peppering us with ideas and questions. She always wanted to know this and that about the hay we would harvest, the fruit we would pick, or the trees she would watch us fell. She could be exhausting, especially since Vic and I had no interest in knowing anything about our jobs except what we had to do and how much we would earn.

But we missed her with every mile. We were two dogs without a master.

Is it not true that the landscape of our lives changes depending on the company we keep? A co-worker who throws you under the bus plunges you into an ocean so salty you float. An abusive father spreads his power over the deadly and frozen nighttime peaks of the Rockies. A lover takes you to a lush valley and surrounds you with protective hills. And Teeny. Teeny put us in mind of an Amazon rainforest, with its infinite and irrepressible colors and sounds.

We hitched and walked all day and waited hours for a train, then hopped into a boxcar, pulled in by a gang of boys about our age. We were headed into the belly of the dustbowl.

I want you to hold an image of the Big Trouble in your mind, so let me tell you of Kansas. It suffered just north of Oklahoma, bordering misery with more misery. We rode all night and pulled into Wichita. A parade of unimaginable pain welcomed us as we got our bearings.

There were men laying just up a berm from the tracks, a bundle or cap for a pillow. Families huddled outside makeshift tents on the side of the road. Women sat on suitcases outside jalopies while the men shared cigarettes and talked of north, south, west, or east.

For as far as we could see—if we were inclined to look, which I am ashamed to say we were not—there were the infamous Hoovervilles. They had popped up along streams and under bridges—a sprawling stain of makeshift shacks born of dump-scavenged corrugated metal, cardboard, and tin cans flattened to the size of a roof tile. The old goat President Hoover had already been booted out. But his negligence was everywhere.

What I see to this day are the faces. Expressionless eyes diverted in shame. Mouths that once laughed and joked were puckered and dry. Jaw lines and cheekbones jutted out of skin so dry it begged for hydration.

Vic took me to a jungle that first night in Wichita. It fed on its inhabitants, for it demanded flesh and dignity from everyone who crossed into it. The mass desperation stretched as far as I could see. Toddlers and babies clung to mothers who had nothing to feed them. Little shirts and trousers, the size of my arm, hung by threads on emaciated bodies.

A jungle is like any place: one is the same as another, except some are big, some are small.

Go. Go to your grocery store. Who do you see there? The same people I see when my granddaughter ferries me to town on Saturday mornings. Children wriggling in carts screaming for cereal, or at the checkout line, fingers in noses, demanding candy. In the aisles. There. It's the old woman in the crowded snack aisle who moves so slowly you have to walk in stuttered half steps behind her, not yet realizing you'll join her one day. The man on his phone who talks too loudly so you'll think he's a doctor or stockbroker. The hippie couple in homemade sandals touching every single tomato in the organic section. And among the one hundred shoppers in the store—for statistics dictate this—one murderer or molester.

Take away the grocery store and replace it with a grove of trees. In the jungle there were whiners, bullies, braggarts, misers, dreamers, the old and the lame, the malevolent, and those who had just plain given up.

Vic took me on tours of the seedy side of the Big Trouble during the weeks before we returned to collect Teeny. We went to a Salvation Army mission in Garden City, where everything was dried up among weeds and thorns. All the men called it Sally. I called it hell. Vic showed me how to tie my shoes and rucksack to my person, lest they be stolen in the night.

Cattle we were. Nameless. Faceless. They gave us numbered cards to exchange for a meal and a cot. But first they fumigated us like animals. Herded us into one thought, which was we should be grateful for what we received.

And we were. Pride is a fleeting thing when you are hungry and dirty. And it was nice to be thoroughly clean, if only for the time it took you to hear this sentence.

If we had set foot in a shelter with Teeny, she would have been whisked away and every effort made to send her home. Even if she had cut her hair and played the boy, she was discoverable. Her every cell and pore gave her away.

Now, what of the bullies and marauders who parade in grocery stores and jungles? The cheap and the mean? Worst of all, what of the hopeless? On those summer nights Vic and I stopped in the jungles, the hopeless girls arrived after dark. I saw them float in, wisps of broken humanity. They had the reddish complexions that identified them as Oklahoma clay-eaters. Like their Okie cousins, neighbors, and friends, they had succumbed at some point to swallowing the red clay earth just to silence their stomachs.

Can. Can you pinpoint, like a tack on a map, the exact moment your innocence was lost? Remember, I was twelve. What did I know of girls leading men behind bushes? What did I know of scraggly tramps counting their coins around a fire? Not for a meal or a bed. Or five meals, for that is what fifty cents would get you those days. Vic had to explain the girls to me, and the primordial need to trade fifty cents for a woman's touch. Or a girl's. For they were girls. Like Teeny. I turned away from it all, as if my back could make it all go away.

Colorado wasn't much better. You've been there. To that place where you travel from bad to worse and back again. Perhaps you are there now. I am not, but the memory of this is a scratch on my mind's eye.

Many farmers employed regular workers who came back year after year, so we were lucky to find work, as Vic was one of the regulars. When the trucks came for us, we walked past hundreds of men waiting for any leftover jobs. We all pretended not to see each other. Us to assuage our guilt, them to hide their shame.

We bent over the earth twelve hours a day for three weeks. I worked alongside children I knew were starving, but who could outpace me. We got fifty cents a day and a spot to pitch a tent in a migrant camp so foul, we took our chances sleeping in the farmer's fields. There was little food to speak of. Bounty, bounty, everywhere and not a bite to eat.

How many footprints did I leave around those strawberry plants? There is no way of knowing. One step was as meaningless as another, and it did not warrant thinking about.

That was the thing of our journey because no matter how many steps we took, ours was a circular, never-ending voyage.

Chapter Seven

Our reunion with Teeny was nothing like our separation. She did not know the exact day of our return, nor did we. When she saw us coming up the road, she ran to meet us, and flew into Vic's surprised arms (they didn't know what to do), and then into mine. She squeezed me like I was a rag or sponge. My arms knew to squeeze back. She felt like a baby hummingbird when she leaned against my chest, and I heard her heartbeat, like fluttering wings.

She whispered into my shirt, the words came tumbling out in one long breath: "I'm so glad you're back you don't know how I missed you and that mean old cow never did take her eyes off me not for one minute like she just knew I was stealing from their larder but I never did you know I never would not even when I was hungry."

We were muscled, tanned, and hard-scrabbled from the picking. Her skin was the color of caramel from tending the vegetable garden. She chattered like a child about the baby and the money she had saved to share with us. The farmer's wife and the daughter, holding the baby, stood on the front porch and met us with far less enthusiasm. Seems in the time it took for Teeny to run out and meet us, they had put her belongings in her rucksack and packed three sack lunches, however meagre.

We walked for half a day down country roads. Our sack lunches were gone by dinner. It was getting cool. We settled in a grove of trees. I found firewood, Teeny foraged for berries and nuts and Vic caught a trout in a nearby stream, which flowed next to a "No Trespassing" sign nailed to a tree.

We had pitifuls to eat—sharing one fish, berries and wild nuts between us without benefit of Jesus' miracles. And there were not enough nuts that year to harvest and sell. But you must see, we were a content and festive band. We were together again, and our stomachs would not complain and wake us up in the middle of the night.

We passed through Des Moines, a small city that was—like every other city—choked with men in lines and on street corners. Vic couldn't abide a line.

"Besides," he said, "those men and boys there in that line. They're local. The missions and relief ain't gonna give us squat until every one of those bellies is full."

He waved his arm down the long line and we looked to the end of his fingers for his explanation.

You will hear of Des Moines again, though I did not know it then.

We stopped in the alleys, picking through the trash without finding a scrap. Some other poor soul had been there before us. Teeny ran ahead and squealed when she opened the last can. We were instantly by her side. I imagined bruised fruit or a loaf of stale bread, for we were behind a diner. Teeny's squeal brought the unwanted attention of the cook, who slammed out of the door and threw a bucket of water on us. Vic and I scat but Teeny dropped her hand into the can and snatched something out, which she promptly pocketed before running after us.

"You can't do that, Teeny," Vic scolded. "There's already enough attention on us. Don't bring anymore, you hear?"

"Aww, Vic," I started to protest in her defense, but he shot me down with an elbow in my ribs.

But Teeny was not listening to us. She was admiring her find— a small silver lady's make-up compact. How could I tell, you wonder? Well, I wasn't a total heathen, you remember. My mother had had one, and they were sold in Hoffman's Drugstore back home. Teeny opened it and admired her face in the cracked mirror. There was no powder, but she was charmed none-the-less. She peered at herself and ran a pinky along an eyebrow, as if she was smoothing a tiny wrinkle on a bedsheet.

We walked into the neighborhoods looking for a house to hit. We might see a house with clothes on a line and toys in the yard. If there was no car, that meant either there wasn't one, or the man was at work. Teeny knocked at such a house. The lawn was not mowed and the fence gate was broken.

A bedraggled woman, a baby on her hip and two toddlers clinging to her leg, answered the door, as if with the last ounce of energy and spirit she possessed. Each child was naked save for dirty underthings. The woman wore a stained flour sack dress with a straggly hem. She looked as poor as us.

Teeny made her appeal, as Vic had shown her, telling the woman that she and her brothers would work for a meal. She was quick on her feet with a story, and I was certain she was offering the exhausted mother a reprise from those children. Teeny, it turned out, was good with children. Maybe because she was so small herself.

After a minute, she turned from the stoop and waved us to come on.

"Well, I don't have much, but enough to share, I 'spose," the woman sighed. "It's just beans and biscuits and coffee without sugar. Mostly chicory really."

We stood in her kitchen, almost so empty I expected to find my echo hiding in a corner. The room had been stripped of its typical wares. There was one pot on the stove, bubbling the beans she had offered. On the table sat four bowls, four spoons and two chipped coffee cups.

We surveyed her destitution, and she surveyed ours.

"My man's been gone looking for work," she explained, the children still attached to her. "I've had to sell what I don't need just to get by." She grinned weakly. "But you can see I need some help 'round here."

Vic tackled the yard while I fixed the gate. We fixed the chicken coop together. There was no fresh straw, so we just fluffed what was already there, for what little good that did. Inside, Teeny gathered the children in the kitchen and washed them one by one in a large wooden half barrel. They were transfixed by her singing.

"She'll be coming 'round the mountain when she comes. She'll be driving six white horses when she comes. She'll be wearing silk pajamas when she comes, when she comes. She'll be coming 'round the mountain when she comes."

And on and on. Soon, the two toddlers were singing with her while the baby splashed and laughed. The exhausted mother had disappeared upstairs, probably for a lie-down.

When we had finished, the lawn mown, repairs made and children clean, we set them on the crates around the table and Teeny dished out the beans and collected the biscuits from the pie safe.

The children wolfed down their food as if they were half starved, which they were, I supposed. Their faces made the movement of eating, but their bellies would not be filled.

We looked on as Teeny fed the baby—sitting on her lap—one bean at a time, one crumb of biscuit at a time so as to not choke it. In one of my rare flashes into the future, I imagined Teeny in a pretty dress and starched white apron, sitting in her own kitchen. She morphed from the rebellious, petulant teenager into a little mother fussing over her charges. She gleamed, like the shine on the appliances. I imagined that the child in her lap would have the same red flame locks. In my mind, it played with a yo-yo. Like the one I had traded to Bo Wrinkles.

While the children ate, we took half of what we considered a fair portion for our work, leaving what looked like enough for their next meal. What they would do after that I did not know.

After Teeny had washed and dried the dishes, we each took a turn washing our hands and necks in the cold and murky bath water where Teeny had bathed the children. You would have turned your nose up at it, and you would have been right to do so. Those babies were as dirty as we were, and God knows they probably peed in that water easy as can be. But it did the trick, and we were more presentable than when we had arrived.

By that time, it was early afternoon. We had been there four hours and it was time to find a jungle before the sun and moon swapped places. Teeny crept up the stairs and ten minutes later returned with the woman, who looked somewhat more put together in a clean dress and hair pulled back with combs. She had painted a thin slash of red lipstick on her weak smile.

"You were Godsends, you were," she told us, looking at her children, sitting on the couch with the baby asleep between the toddlers.

"We thank you ma'am for sharing your meal with us," Vic said, and Teeny and I echoed a chorus of "Thank you, ma'ams."

The woman hugged Teeny with arms and tears, not wanting to let go.

"God bless you. You are but children yourselves. May the Lord look out for you."

This made us uncomfortable, as the Lord had done nothing for us, and certainly had done far less for this woman and her hungry children.

We left the same way we had come, by the kitchen door, the screen now tight and affixed to its frame. As we passed the table, I saw that Vic had left a one-dollar bill in the middle. He was tight with our money, and despite the coins and bills in his jacket, we sometimes went two days without food. Vic wouldn't let us starve, but he wasn't past letting us go hungry. At the sight of that dollar bill, my throat caught and damn if that woman's tears didn't show up in my own eyes.

Back in town, we came upon a drugstore and Teeny darted in before we could stop her. We loitered outside, talking with a boy who stopped to chat. He was a handsome sort, with dark hair trimmed so short it looked as if it must have hurt. His clothes were cleaner than ours, but also patched over and over. Like us, he had wound string around his shoes, and cardboard peaked out the sides.

"Which way you boys headed?" he asked with a smile that told too much and too little at the same time. His voice was like Teeny's, a drawl so long and slow it reminded me of molasses.

She came out just then, laughing and skipping like a little girl, shoving something small into her pocket. All of a sudden I saw her through the boy's eyes. Yes, you are right. She still wore the same dirty work pants and frayed shirt we had gotten for her in Pittsburgh. But her cap sat at a jaunty angle, red flame curls springing forth, and her belt cinched tight to reveal a waist. Vic and I saw, for the first time, the enchantment we looked at every day. The boy doffed his cap at a surprised Teeny, then turned and walked away, whistling.

Boys like him thronged in gangs along the rails, creating an inevitable chaos atop the cars and when they jumped on and off the trains. They moved as one, a sea of torn pants and sweaters unraveling at the elbows. There was always a leader, and it was he who decided when to red light some poor soul, which meant asking him to watch for the crossing lights, and then booting him out of the boxcar when his back was turned. Some of these boys watched as the old 'boes rode between cars, or slipped underneath a car to ride the rods, which were the underbelly metal scaffolding, and imitated them. This was a surefire way to get killed, and we never attempted these risky moves. We kept our distance from the gangs of boys, and the frenzy they whipped up with dust and shouts. If they appeared in the jungles in smaller groups of three or four, we would share a meal and talk of the road, exchanging the same information we all looked for—where to go, what was there, how to survive. When they appeared in droves and threw rocks and cursed the jungle buzzards, we fled. Really, they were no better than the bulls.

Vic guided us through town toward the tracks that afternoon, but the throngs of boys deterred us, and each day for a week we chose to try our luck on the road. We left the rails for later, and we walked and hitched through northern Iowa and the Dakotas.

Remember I told you that on the road we met with kindness, but sometimes with the kind of evil you never forget?

Let me tell you now of inhumanity. For that is the worst kind of evil.

September was closing in on itself, but there was still time to get to Oregon to pick peas for a few weeks if we hurried. As we walked, the road dust billowing behind us, a big woman dressed in a dingy white housedress stopped us at the edge of her property. We stared at her over her fence. I know what all of us were thinking. We were thinking of our stomachs, for they were empty. She had the pudgy, clammy, sour feel of someone who did not have the energy or inclination to finish farm chores. Which was just fine by us.

"Say now, you fellas hungry?" she asked.

"Yes, ma'am," Vic answered. For he often spoke on our behalf. You can guess, can't you, that I did not?

"We will work for food if you have any odd jobs for us. You can see we're big and strong." He motioned to me and then Teeny. "And she here can help you in the kitchen. She's a bang-up gal with canning."

"Is she now?" the woman said, looking at Teeny with slit eyes.

"Best come in, raggedy though you are. I've got a whole mess of things needs doin'. I'll put out your supper while you work."

We filed through the gate as she held it. I smelled sweat and perfume as I passed her and wondered how the two could co-exist.

After she had instructed us, she walked toward the house and Teeny started to follow, but the woman cut her off.

"No missy, you're not coming into my house. Not now, not ever. You go over there and snap those beans."

She gave Teeny a nasty smirk, and a knot clenched in my stomach. Something was not right.

I began to spread manure from a pile half as tall as me. Vic was on his knees in the garden, pulling weeds, and Teeny was snapping beans, sitting on a barrel, trying to balance a basket and bowl.

As we worked, the woman placed food on the table. I saw that there were sandwiches wrapped in wax paper and a basket of deviled eggs nestled in a cloth napkin. A pile of small cookies sat in a dented red tin that once held a rum-soaked Christmas fruit cake. It was not a feast, but it was more than enough for the three of us. We hadn't had a good meal like that in days. The woman had a matronly bulk that slowed her down, but she was dutifully delivering the promised food. I could practically taste it. I did not want to get my hopes up, but I secretly hoped for oatmeal cookies specked with raisins.

When she caught me staring, she shouted at me, even though I was only ten feet away.

"When you've got that mess spread I need fresh straw in the chicken coop. You girl, give those beans to me and go help them."

I am not ashamed to say that by this time all of us were so weak from hunger that we could barely finish our chores. I saw stars when I bent over to spread fresh straw and had to steady myself. Teeny was so lethargic, I told her to just lean on the wall while I worked.

Finally, we were done, and we gathered around the porch, hungry for our well-earned supper.

The woman stood on the steps, an old cow, blocking our way.

"You did a piss poor job on your chores. You're nothing but some lazy bums."

"We're sure sorry, ma'am, that you aren't pleased with our

work," Vic said. He was too tired and weak to argue. "Perhaps we could have a bite and then can keep working. A meal would perk us right up and we'll do everything right. You'll see."

She laughed, and howled, and her belly and chins shook.

"You think I'm going to pay a bunch of worthless tramps like you?"

Then she rearranged her face as a car drove up and parked mere feet from us. A man, tall and robust and wearing the white collar of a priest, emerged with an old fruit crate and the old cow was suddenly all penny candy and soda pop. The two exchanged pleasantries about the weather. Then the priest claimed our meal from the front porch, the old cow packing it into his crate. We watched in disbelief as our hard-earned meal was spirited away. After the car was gone, we looked back at the old cow. She had poured herself a long, tall glass of lemonade and drank it down in one large gulp. We watched a small yellow stream of liquid drizzle out of her mouth, down her chin and onto her dress.

You see her, this evil thing, don't you? You've seen the likes of her before, in your own life. The teacher who gave you bad marks because you were poor and dirty. The schoolyard bully who ground your face into the dirt with his foot. The waiter who swore you gave him a ten-dollar bill when you know it was a fifty, because it was payday, and you were celebrating with an early morning pastry and coffee.

When we had cleared the woman's property, Vic took out his *Reader's Digest* and made a note to stay clear of this farm. Then he took a piece of chalk from his bag and marked that lady's fence with the symbol of danger. It was not like him to use that symbol. But I suppose evil and danger are two sides of the same coin, and so I understood why.

In the jungle that night we warned the other 'boes.

"I coulda told you that, boy," the jungle buzzard said, and laughed. He reminded me of Bo Wrinkles, except he had teeth. "If she were a snake she'd be a rattler, all right."

"But there weren't any signs," I declared, incredulous at the oversight.

The old man shrugged. "Rain must have got it. Best carve them signs in the trees."

We had little for the pot that night. We had saved a few pocketfuls of nuts. Again, Teeny offered a story. She had the power to bewitch. Had Vic or I tried that, we would have been booted out.

"But we all three eat," she said, nodding to us. "Me and my brothers."

No one responded, so she began, and Vic and I settled in to hear her gypsy tale a second time. But she surprised us, as she would again and again.

"Nineteen years ago, when you all had jobs and homes or went to school, a baby was abandoned at a convent called St. Mary's. It was cloistered high in the Smoky Mountains of Tennessee, where fog always out runs the sun. Because they were on their own, the nuns were unaccustomed to visitors, much less babies. They lived in a compound of three stone buildings, one for work, one for sleep, and one, of course, for prayer. It had been more than fifty years since someone had abandoned a baby on their doorstep."

"What's cloister?" one of the 'boes asked.

She always answered us patiently and kindly, like we were children. "It means a place that is shuttered from the outside world, where no one comes or goes."

"What's shuttered?" someone else asked, and we all shushed him.

"Shuttered means closed off," she said. "Like you close the shutter of a window."

Teeny then continued her story. "Well, on that morning in June, when the Mother Superior opened the gates to retrieve the milk delivery, she saw a squirming baby tucked under a blanket in an old wooden fruit crate.

"Oh my," she gasped, and crossed herself.

Teeny made the motion with her own hand and half a dozen of us did the same.

"It was the way of the sisters of St. Mary's," she continued, "to raise a foundling girl in good Christian fashion. Once she was old enough, she becomes a novice, which is a sister who is practicing, before she can become a full nun, married forever to Christ the Lord.

"The Mother Superior brought the milk and the baby inside the warm convent. So starved was that baby that she drank two bottles, then promptly was sick all over the Mother's long, black habit. But, Mother Superior did not mind in the least. And do you know why?"

We all shook our heads, for we had no earthly idea.

"Well, the previous month the Monsignor came to visit the cloister. He was the only other person allowed into the compound, except for the doctor. The Monsignor is a churchman who lived down in the town and told the women what to do. On his last visit, he told the Mother Superior that her convent was short one sister. You see, to be a cloistered convent in those days, there had to be twelve women. But old Sister Tabitha had died the previous winter. The Monsignor gave Mother Superior two months to find another sister.

"Of course, how was Mother Superior supposed to do that while cloistered away from the world? She thought it right unfair that the Monsignor had put this burden on her. But she was a faithful woman and prayed every day for a miracle, which God saw fit to deliver in the form of an abandoned baby girl, who would one day be the twelfth nun. Of course, it would take fourteen years until the baby could become a novice, but this seemed to satisfy the Monsignor. And the nuns went on tending their vegetables, weaving grape vine baskets to raise money for the poor, and praying on their bare knees ten times a day. Outside their convent walls a war raged on the other side of the world. While the girl grew into a young woman, boys she would never meet went to

France and Germany and died on bloody battlefields she had never heard of.

"When the girl was fourteen, the sisters chopped off her long golden hair and pushed her into the white habit of a novice. Sister James John had spun it from the coarse cotton they grew. From then on, she had to pray ten times a day on her bare knees in the cold stone chapel. She had to weave baskets until her fingers bled. The girl did not want to be a sister of St. Mary's, but what could she do?

"She could wait. That was all, for only the Mother Superior, the Monsignor and the town doctor had keys to the gate. Two years after the girl had been forced into the white habit of a novice, old Sister Marguerite died. The girl knew that the doctor would be sent for, so she tiptoed out of her room and positioned herself by the gate to the property. When he arrived at the gate the old man folded himself out of his car. The key shook in his hand as he turned it in the old lock and pushed open the gate so he could drive through. It was at this moment that the girl escaped and ran far into the woods."

Teeny stopped talking.

"But what happened to her?" someone asked.

"Well, I don't know, now do I?" Teeny said. "No one ever saw her again. She escaped back into the same woods she had come from as a baby."

There were many grumbles and complaints regarding the inadequacy of the tale. But there was nothing to be done, apparently.

"That's quite a story," I remarked, when we had chosen our sleeping spots and were settling down.

"Thank you," she said.

"Was that you in the story? Were you the girl?"

She looked at me, as if insulted. "Of course not."

"Did it close after the girl left?" I asked.

"What?" she inquired, distracted.

"The cloister, of course."

She flicked some dirt off her pants.

"I have no idea."

As we dozed by the fire, there were always some who were up and about so that I never slept a full night through in a jungle. When I awoke with a jolt, Mutt, the youngest 'bo, was still tending the fire so I knew I had not slept long. I glanced next to me. Teeny was awake. In the soft light of a full moon, I could see that she had a bottle of nail polish in one hand and was painting her nails a fire engine red. I wanted to inhabit her mind, for surely in there was the manual that taught her how to thumb her nose at hunger and exhaustion. I realized in that moment the overwhelming difference between the two of us. She was, quite simply, not afraid. Fear was the very fabric of my life those days. Fear and worry. I thought that because I was afraid, she did not have to be.

Chapter Eight

Of course there were times when we were happy, if you can call it that. But you know as well as I that happiness by day is not the same as happiness by night. Perhaps I am trying to tell you that by day we sometimes found ways to entertain ourselves. By night we turned back into pumpkins.

In the towns and cities, when we could make ourselves somewhat presentable, we hit the libraries. In rain or blistering heat, we crept into these vast repositories of knowledge, each disappearing into our own corner.

Teeny read the ladies' magazines, domestic fairytales of a kind. On the road, she would regale us with stories of housework, cookware, and domestic bliss that I was certain she had never experienced. Vic finally told her to stop talking of the strawberry shortcakes, macadamia nut cookies, and fruit pies that she favored. She found glamour in the picture tabloids and mooned over Clark Gable and was dazzled by Katharine Hepburn and Vivien Leigh. We occasionally went to the pictures, but only to get out of the rain, or in the winter if we had to wait hours for a train. Teeny watched, mesmerized, while Vic and I slept through *Pennies from*

Heaven, Shall We Dance, Wee Willie Winkie, and goodness knows what else. We were just glad for a soft, warm place to rest.

In the library, as Teeny read about a world she had never seen, I was drawn to the books that told me who I was: books of science and anatomy. On the pages of these tomes I saw what I really looked like.

Can you guess what Vic read? He who always knew which way was north. He read the news and told us of the world around us. And of course, it was all myth to us. Until we heard it from Vic. Howard Hughes set a new flying record between Los Angeles and New York. Amelia Earhart's aeroplane disappeared in the South Pacific. Floating above New Jersey, the German airship Hindenburg caught fire. These stories, and so many more, were in the air around us. We knew they were true, for they had come from Vic, after all. But just because something is true, does not mean it feels that way. Vic made sure we always knew what day and date it was. He thought this anchored us to the world in a respectable way.

One afternoon, as we picked our way along a desolate highway outside Boise, a woman pulled her long, sleek convertible onto the shoulder, dirt spinning around her tires. She pulled her sunglasses low on her nose the better to peer at us. I could tell by the way Teeny practically hummed with energy that she had instantly noticed the silk scarf that kept the woman's hair from mussing in the wind. Here was Katharine Hepburn, or Vivien Leigh, arrived to rescue us. As we gaped, the woman told us to hop on the running boards and she drove us into the city, pulling up to the curb right in front of a hot dog stall. This woman, in a butter yellow scarf and winged sunglasses, smeared ketchup and mustard on fifteen hot dogs, and in the time it took her to finish one we had each eaten three. She tinkled when she laughed. Despite the mustard on her chin, Teeny did not take her eyes from her own reflection in the woman's sunglasses. The mustard was bright yellow, and the ketchup was a heavy red I could feel in my hand. For the first time in a long time, color ceased to be a punishment.

Red was not an aching back in the tomato fields. Green was not a shuck of corn that demanded to be snapped off its stalk.

And then the woman was gone, as quickly as the hot dogs. She pressed a few bills into Vic's hands, wiped the mustard from Teeny's chin with a handkerchief, and patted my arm.

That was a happy summer, at least in the only way that it could be for us. In the jungles and in city parks, Vic, and sometimes Teeny, read the newspapers other 'boes used for pillows and blankets. Teeny read the parts that Vic set aside: the jokes, advice columns and recipes. She would read us the hobo jokes and then laugh, her tiny frame riddled with the giggles we did not share. But Vic's stern face and my disappointed head shake did not deter her. She could not understand that the hoboes people were laughing at were us. But then, perhaps, she did not think of herself as a 'bo.

In the spring of 1937, we lingered in St. Paul, waiting to catch the Northern Pacific, a hotshot that would take us to Butte where we would switch and then end up in Oregon to pick peas. It was eight hours until the steam engine would chug in, and we were all hungry. This is when Teeny masqueraded us as what we were. In retrospect, I see just how brilliant her plan was, and it was one we would return to several times.

She lay sprawled under a park bench—for that is how small she was—and we heard her exclamation pierce the quiet Vic and I had come to savor, and only experienced in rare moments. She scrambled out and thrust a newspaper under our noses, then snatched it back again and began to read aloud:

"Members of the Beta Gamma chapter of Delta Theta Chi, Class of 1926 and the local Elks and their guests will be delightfully entertained at a hobo party at Beaver Creek Park, this Saturday afternoon. Everyone will be dressed as hoboes, and one lucky bum will be awarded the prize for having the most realistic costume. Guests will enjoy strict hobo-fare. Cost of admission is thirty-five cents to benefit the good works of these outstanding civic groups."

I had seen these notices before, about the kind of people who swam around the Big Trouble instead of through it. And along the way—when they weren't throwing 'boes off trains and rousting us out of jungles—some enjoyed their hobo parties. Fraternities, women's clubs, chambers of commerce and other community booster groups followed the same pattern. Guests were to dress up as hoboes, would enjoy a hobo meal and entertainment, and then prizes would be given for the best costume.

"Oh, but we must go boys," Teeny exclaimed, and thrust the newspaper at us again.

The party was about to begin, and much to our surprise, Vic stood up, tucked in his shirt and headed in that direction. We scrambled to keep up with him, so surprised were we that he had assented in his quiet, brooding way.

"Say there, young man," we heard a man's voice call out as we hit the sidewalk. "Say boy, where do you think you're going?"

Now I think I told you that Vic typically spoke for us. But this time Teeny turned and said sweetly, "Why to the Elks hobo party, sir."

We turned with her and I studied the old man. He wore a gold tie, and a red-jeweled tie pin winked at us. Was he an Elk? Or a Rotarian? For all I knew, he could have been a Shriner or a Mason. It was no matter, for they all looked the same to me, just as we looked the same to them.

For a moment, the old man did not respond, but then he laughed and said, "By Jove, I've not seen such a good hobo since the crash of ninety-eight. One of you will take home the grand prize for certain."

To our horror, Teeny invited him to join us, but he said he was too old for such fanciful pursuits. We watched him amble away from us, and I expected Vic to explode at Teeny's gall, but he did not. He knew we had a long ride ahead of us on the hotshot, and we needed a good meal to sustain us all the way to Montana.

As we approached Beaver Creek Park, small groupings of

costumed 'boes began to arrive, exiting from sporty cars. The ladies removed the fur stoles draped around them and tossed them into the back seats of their cars. The men traded their jaunty hats for headwear that was ripped and torn. We watched them approach the entrance booth, congratulating each other on the magnificence of their costumes. And truth be told, if we had not seen them emerge from their cars, we would not have known otherwise, so authentic were they. But on closer inspection, we would see how clean they actually were. Ah, you see, don't you? The grime of the homeless cannot be imitated, for it is applied over time, not in front of a marble vanity, or walnut framed mirror hanging over a custom-made chest of drawers.

Teeny, Vic, and I loitered nonchalantly at the edge of the park. Each guest presented either a ticket or thirty-five cents before they could be admitted. As I expected, Vic's yellow-topped Viking head moved from side to side, looking for a way in. We saw a group of party guests across the park, mingling and laughing. Vic jerked his head and we followed him around the periphery of the park. It was easy to melt into this small group of costumed hoboes at the back, and they welcomed us with hoots and laughs and slaps on the back, saying, "Ho there, fella, you're going to win for certain" and "Oh, I wish I had thought to scuff my shoes like that."

I knew Vic wanted us to join the food line, eat, and be on our way before we were discovered. But Teeny was having none of it, and once she had begun her masquerade, he could not stop her. She had taken off her hat and let her fiery red hair cascade onto her shoulders. With her clean hands and red nail polish, she could have been one of them. We watched in horror as she approached a group of women, each in torn overalls and kerchiefs around their heads. One was carrying a long stick over her shoulder, with a little bundle bouncing at the end as she laughed and joked.

They stopped talking when Teeny approached and broke into her expert chatter. She told them she was new in town. We watched as the heads turned toward us and Teeny motioned us over, introducing us as her brothers.

"Oh, we need such help, you know," she nattered on. "Can you tell me which is the best beauty parlor and butcher?"

Vic and I managed to drift away as the women started to talk about someone named Loretta, and Teeny nodded her head vigorously. I laughed at the absurdity of it all, but Vic shot me a withering look. I knew Teeny was in for it.

Vic and I joined the line and were amused to see that the dinner was a bowl of stew and a hunk of crusty bread. We did not complain and went back for seconds. Before too long Teeny wandered over and enjoyed a bowl. While Teeny ate, Vic shielded me and I lifted bread and shoved pieces into my pockets.

Vic insisted that we leave, but Teeny wanted to stay for the prizes. I believe she thought one of us might win. Not wanting to make a scene, Vic let her have her way.

There was much laughter and carrying on as the prizes were given. Third prize went to the woman with the stick and bundle. A man in a torn suit with a five-day stubble was second. The grand prize went to a hobo so real I felt he must be one of us. He was thin, like the 'boes we'd harvested hay with, and he had an ache in his eyes that could see through me if he had looked my way. His suit hung loosely and was ripped in all the right places. But then he was introduced as the local bank president, and suddenly I saw the gold watch upon his wrist and the high shine on his shoes. Ah, it was a trick of my mind, seeing only what it always saw. As I watched him collect his prize (a tomato, bar of soap, and new socks, all bundled into a smart red kerchief), I wondered if there were others, like us, in attendance. It was impossible to tell.

This would not be our only hobo party, for we were emboldened by the hot stew with real meat and sweet baby carrots. And I can still taste the sweetness of the green peas that polka dotted those delicious meals.

On that evening, as angry as Vic was, he did not explode at

Teeny as I expected him to. Later, I realized why he had not chastised her. Our bellies were full. We had secured an empty boxcar on the hotshot and could sleep for hours, warm and safe. Well, as safe as we could be. For the first time since we had joined forces, Vic had help taking care of us. And himself.

We rode the Northern Pacific through Montana, and it was here that we crossed paths again with that handsome boy from outside the drugstore, who introduced himself as Roley. He hopped into our car at Butte, and the first thing he did was doff his cap at Teeny, and give a slight bow, just as he had done in Iowa. It was a gesture of intimate recognition, and it made my skin crawl. Say. If he sat next to you on a bus, you would suck in your gut and straighten your shoulders and say he could have been a picture in a Sears catalog. You would admire his straight, white teeth. Like Chicklets gum.

With Roley in tow—for Teeny had insisted he come with us, which he agreed to without hesitation—we found our way to a pea farm in Oregon and the grower hired the four of us at fifteen cents a bushel. This was the most pitiful wage we had come by. But that is all the farmer had to give and we took it.

We squatted bent over in the pea fields for hours, working to a poetic rhythm that we heard only on our backs. Day after day, Roley did the unexpected, and worked circles around us. For every pea he picked, he put one in Teeny's basket. Vic and I exchanged enough looks to fill an ocean.

When the four of us gathered in the evenings, Roley sat beside Teeny, as if he had earned the right. Remember. Remember when you met a person who told you, without words or motion, not to trust them. This person sends a silent missive in the squint of the eyes or with the angle of a chin.

If only it had been that easy with Roley. But we could not articulate the concerns that consumed us. All we could do was watch. Watch him preen. Watch him slip syrupy words into Teeny's orbit. Watch her smile. Watch her demure. We none of us had much to give, yet he always produced some treat or another for her. A hard-boiled egg. A dime he found in the bushes. A lace-trimmed handkerchief that had belonged to his mother.

Can you see? Roley was the worst kind of thief, for his gifts were delivered with ill intentions.

For those weeks in the Oregon pea fields, we had settled on a patch of land surrounded by a grove of trees, away from the migrant families who pitched their tents and parked their jalopies by the stream. We relished this reprieve from the mewling babies and children who fairly hummed with hunger.

Roley was older than all of us, with steel-like edges that sharpened into sarcasm and an unkindness that he managed to hide from Teeny. He was called Roley, he said, because he used to travel with a mongrel stray, a shabby little beagle terrier mix who was devoted to him. On the streets of Omaha, he commanded the dog as it performed its repertoire of tricks. He was famous for his rollover. On command, the pup would fall to the ground when his master pointed a finger gun and said, "Bang." The dog would writhe in pretend frenzied agony then roll over three times before it stopped, playing dead.

We had been sitting around the fire when Roley told that story, except for Teeny, who was behind a bush just out of earshot. Vic asked what had happened to the dog. Roley carelessly flicked his cigarette into the fire, making it spit.

"Oh," he declared, "I couldn't feed it when I left the city. No one wanted to see a trick dog in the country, so I hung it from a tree."

Teeny came back to the campfire just after Roley had finished his horrendous tale of the poor dog. He patted the earth beside him. She sat down and sighed contentedly.

With no more picking to be had, and September now on speaking terms with October, it was time to think about how to get through the winter. Vic knew a tomato farmer in Salinas. The pay was terrible, but there would be hearty meals on which to feast, and then we would catch a freighter back east to Florida. It was while we were packing up to leave Oregon that Vic and I understood that Roley meant to go with us.

That night I committed my first and only act of violence. When Teeny was fast asleep—her telltale snorts and sighs penetrating the darkness—Vic grabbed Roley by the legs, while I shoved a bandana into his mouth. Vic pulled him out of his bedroll and onto his feet. He tied his hands behind him with a rope and prodded him to move forward.

At the stream, away from any other soul, Vic pushed him down on his knees and thrust his face into the water, holding his head down long enough to almost kill him. Then he pulled Roley's head up so he could struggle for a few breaths of air before he dunked him again. After ten minutes or so of this, we left Roley sprawled, sputtering and crying, on his back on the grass next to the stream.

No. He was not dead. Do not think that of me. I became a healer and took an oath to relieve suffering. But that was years to come yet. Surely you can see that we had to stop Roley. Do you remember when I bid you study the personalities of humanity? Remember that one in one hundred is a murderer or molester? That was Roley.

Chapter Nine

Teeny did not talk to us for the next two days. We hopped a Union Pacific boxcar heading to California and she sat as far away as she could, turning her back toward us. She knew we had encouraged Roley to take his leave, having convinced herself that he would never have left without saying good-bye and doffing his cap.

In the end, we told her the story of the dog. She was still sitting with her back to us, and I watched her bony shoulders rise and fall in time to the sobs that wracked her. She flung herself into my arms and sobbed on my shoulder.

"Oh, but how could he?" she sobbed. "It's too wretched."

She slumped against me, and I stroked her hair and put my arm around her.

"I'm sorry," she whispered. "Honest, I am."

I shushed her and told her all would be well.

In that moment I was father, brother, kindly uncle, friend. How could I be all those things to her? Because she needed me to be, of course. My connection to her ran the full spectrum of love, but mostly it traveled only one way.

I thought that day, as we bounced on the filthy, splintery

boards of the boxcar, that I had almost killed to protect her. Or at the very least, I was party to it. This epiphany straightened my back and strained the muscles in my jaw.

In the afternoon, she and Vic sat cross-legged in front of the open boxcar door, watching the world go by. As we barreled west, Teeny tilted her face to the sun, singing softly as she plaited her hair.

In California, Vic's tomato grower turned us away, telling us he was growing only half his usual crop. Times were hard for everyone, it seemed. Even for the ones who grew the food they couldn't sell. He sent us down to the San Fernando Valley to a grower friend with a full crop. With his recommendation we were sent into the tomato rows for ten cents an hour.

We worked alongside the Okies and the Mexicans who fared worse than us. They worked under the added burden of universal hatred. Their mass migration was spit upon at the California border. I suspect they made less than us, though they needed more to feed their children.

You have heard all this, surely. About the hundreds of thousands who took Route 66 west, looking for work in California. They had so many names: Okies, dust bowl gypsies, poor white trash. Trash. Imagine.

The grower offered us little in the way of food, and out in the middle of nowhere, where were we to get sustenance unless we stole it? The grower's daughters delivered stale bread, spoiled vegetables, and bruised apples. At night, Vic and I took turns roaming the neighboring fields and barns to scrounge fresh vegetables, eggs, and whatever else we could find. If we were lucky, we caught a fish or killed a pigeon. We did not have a pot, but we shared our finds with a family of Okies that did.

Vic instructed Teeny and me with hand signals and exaggerated eye movements to take just enough to stop the rumblings in our bellies. As if to say, "There are children here. We must help them."

Go. Go to your kitchen cupboard. Open it and count your

pots and pans. Open the door wider so I can see. Ahh. Three. Four. Five. Six. Small. Medium. Large. Like my daughter and granddaughter, you have Calphalon, Cuisinart, Le Creuset. Now you will see these with the new eyes I have given you. Smile. You have treasures in your midst. You cannot live without owning a pot. And now, neither can I.

We did not work on Sundays for the grower did not believe in toiling on the Sabbath. A good Christian man, he was content to drive past his hungry workers on his way to church, rather than anger his maker. On such a day, many of us still lingered by the fire after another meatless stew. Then Teeny instructed the children to settle into stillness, and offered up a story, as if it was a lemon meringue pie.

And how different her stories tasted, from one tale to another. All the words came from Teeny's mouth but that didn't mean they were hers. These words did not mean that we could know her.

"Let me tell you the story of the raffle baby," she began. "She was born years and years ago in a little town high in the Great Smoky Mountains of Tennessee. Back then, before the Big Trouble, there were do-gooders in this small town who had enough in their larders and closets to provide for others. In particular, there was rich old Mrs. Langhorne, who had grown sick and feeble with a failing heart and stayed in most days. Still, she directed her house girl to dress her in the pretty suits and smart dresses of a long-ago life. For her seamstress had let them out, and each day Mrs. Langhorne struggled into her brassiere, girdle, and stockings like a hippo might. It took them two hours to get her dressed, to curl and set her hair, and paint on her eyebrows. But Mrs. Langhorne insisted on this every day, and, of course, was obliged."

Here Vic interrupted. "Teeny, could you skip the parts about the ladies' undergarments? We here aren't accustomed to that talk and it makes us uncomfortable."

We laughed because Vic blushed full on red. When speaking to Teeny in a more formal manner, he chose his words as if he were delivering them to her on a silver platter. I thought he might be sweet on her, but he never let it show. We were her self-appointed brothers and guardians. She was Snow White and we were her valiant and loyal dwarfs.

When the laughter died down, Teeny continued.

"The Reverend of the Methodist church came every Sunday afternoon to give communion, for Mrs. Langhorne was a descendent of the town's founder and had the money to command the presence of anyone she wanted. Folks knew if they didn't abide her commands she wouldn't give them a Virginia ham at Christmastime or fund the annual church ice cream social.

"One Sunday afternoon, the Reverend lingered longer than usual and ran his finger around his white collar until Mrs. Langhorne asked him to speak his mind.

"He was in a pickle, he said, and made a turn around the room, pausing at the grand piano, then returning to the chair opposite Mrs. Langhorne.

"Two weeks before, the fire chief had presented him with an abandoned baby as if he, Reverend Gladstone Walter, knew what to do with it. Fortunately, his spinster sister lived with him and she accepted the task of caring for the little girl. The baby had been left on the fire station steps. Only a yellow blanket covered the little mite.

"Mrs. Langhorne's mind went not to concern for the baby. No, her first thought was how on earth had she not heard of this from her house girl, who seemed always to bring her the best gossip. Why had no one told her before? It was her right to know.

"The Reverend, unaware of Mrs. Langhorne's wandering mind, continued his story. He had tried, discreetly, to find a good Christian home but to no avail. A wider net needed to be cast, he said. He had consulted the Ladies' Aide Society and no one wanted to give the sweet baby girl to an orphanage or social worker. For she was the sweetest baby. If they handled the adoption through the church, they would ensure that the baby went to a good Christian home, and most importantly, a known family. The Ladies' Aide Society (with the gentle directing of the Reverend, who had misused church donations for a trip to Charlotte) had suggested a raffle. The baby would go to a good home and funds would be raised for a new organ and a tent for the summer revival, the Reverend said. Inwardly, he sighed with relief as he knew he could pilfer from the raffle proceeds to cover his original theft.

"At first, Mrs. Langhorne was horrified. Wasn't such a proposition wholly unchristian? But then she thought of those couples, like she and her Jasper, that could not have children. And of the good impression she would make if she led the effort to find a good home for the babe.

"The Reverend had the church basement swept and volunteered a carpenter to build a small stage from plywood. The ladies of the church made the list of refreshments and assigned baked goods like dealing a game of cards. Only they didn't play cards, of course. The newspaperman printed advertisements and promotional signs. And Mrs. Langhorne paid for it all. She chose the other raffle prizes and attached a high price to the tickets so the mountain people and Melungeons couldn't buy one.

"The grand prize was, of course, the baby, but Mrs. Langhorne decided a radio would be given away, too, and it was put on display in the newspaper print shop window for all to see. A sign sat on top and read, 'Buy Your Tickets Here.'"

Here Teeny paused and yawned dramatically, bending her neck backward making her flaming hair move like a rustling curtain. She knew we were spellbound and itching to hear more. She liked to play with us that way.

"And then what?" someone asked.

The silence that followed was dense like a spice fig cake. We waited for her to go on, but she didn't.

"Well, what about the baby?" I asked, impatient for the rest of the story. It was getting dark and we had crawled under our blankets. It was Vic's turn to watch the fire for the first few hours and then it would be my turn. I desperately wanted to sleep. But more than that I suppose, I didn't want her words to end. For they connected us, you see. She gave. I received.

She yawned again and said, "Tomorrow. I promise I'll finish tomorrow."

I stayed awake thinking that surely it was not a coincidence that all of her stories were set in Tennessee. I saw the outline of the state in my mind, a parallelogram of mountains and fog.

I watched Teeny through the fading light. I could see her take a rag to her hands, spitting on it to rub off the dirt and grime that settled into our knuckles and under our fingernails. When she was done, she brought out the bottle of nail polish and silver compact. First, she examined her face, using a pinky finger to smooth an eyebrow, as I had seen her do before. Next, she picked up the nail polish and slowly unscrewed the top. She drew out the brush and just held it there, hovering above the bottle neck, watching the liquid drip back into the bottle. Then in a flash, she returned the brush and screwed the top back on. The items disappeared back into her pockets. And she lay down, disappearing from my line of sight.

I was reminded of the magpie that is drawn to shiny things, even something as small as your eyelash. It takes its prize in its beak and retreats. Later, you will hear its triumphant caw caw, then see it swoop down again in search of other glittery rewards. Back and forth, back and forth. Looking for silver. Looking for coin. Like all of us in the jungle, I supposed.

Chapter Ten

I awoke thinking of the story from the previous evening. Of the extravagance of Teeny's words. Of the boldness that propelled her make-believe. I knew she would not finish the story until we had settled for the night. First, we would have to carry that day on our backs like rocks, the red tomatoes more hardship than nourishment. We joined the sea of dirty pickers in the fields. When had the ache of a stooped back become rote, I wondered.

Around the fire that evening, Teeny unfurled the rest of the story.

"Mrs. Langhorne wrote a cryptic article for the newspaper to advertise the church raffle. She could not bring herself to come straight out and say the raffle prize was a human baby, but she felt with great satisfaction that she got the point across. She held her breath on the day the article appeared, and let it out three days later, when she was satisfied that it had not caused a disturbance.

"Curiosity spurred raffle ticket sales. The buzz around town was that it was not a real baby, but still, people were intrigued. You had to buy a raffle ticket if you wanted a seat, you see.

"On the night of the program, the town's people—the ones

who could afford a ticket—arrived in droves. Oh my, how fine those women were, as if Easter had come early that year. A charity function was a suitable enough event for the dresses and hats that only saw the streets a few times a year.

"Even the people from the hollers came, but of course they didn't buy raffle tickets, not needing another screaming baby to feed. They could not find even a penny for admission, and instead they clustered outside the Methodist church. They just came to see. Came to see the fuss that was made over an unknown lonesome soul, when no one ever thought of the hunger in their own babies' bellies."

Teeny shook her head just then, and we knew she was pausing, as she often did, to let the sting of inhumanity wash over us. She wanted us to know, she told us many times, about the good and the bad in the world. Like we hadn't seen it for ourselves.

"But if you were the baby, how come you know all this 'bout the fancy dresses and the prizes?" one migrant man asked.

It was then I realized that sometimes Teeny's audiences assumed she had a starring role in her stories. Not many I would guess, but I looked at my companions with different eyes then, wondering who believed. Teeny never let on one way or another when people asked. She liked the mystery of it. Just as I liked the mystery of her.

Another migrant worker shushed the man. "Because the folks who got her told her 'bout it, of course. Now stop interruptin'."

Teeny continued with a wink that seemed to say that she was the raffle baby at the same time it said she was not.

"Now where was I? Oh yes, the finery.

"You never saw such colors fluttering around the church basement like hummingbirds. Everyone was a twitter, even the men. But they tried their best not to show it."

"Didn't them worry 'bout another mouth to feed?" inquired a mother, whose three half-starved children sat around her.

"Well, if they did they wouldn't have bought a raffle ticket," Teeny said sharply, but not unkindly, and then continued.

"So, the lights flickered in the basement and the twittering stopped and everyone sat in the folded chairs, 'cept those who came late and had to stand in the back.

"The Reverend appeared at the front of the room and gave the blessing and talked of the new organ and summer revival. The church choir sang. A little troupe of girls in white dresses filed into the room and stood next to the piano. The Reverend's spinster sister started to play, and the girls opened their mouths for the national anthem. Everyone scuttled to their feet again, and the audience rushed through the tune to be over with it and on with the business at hand.

"The old spinster ushered the girls off the stage. The moment had come. The Reverend escorted old Mrs. Langhorne from her folding chair in the front row onto the makeshift stage, where she sat in an armchair that had been placed there just for the old matriarch. After she was settled, she dipped her hand into the basket that one of the church ladies placed in her lap.

"And she began to speak, feeble at first, but stronger with each ticket she produced, and called it out.

"'For our first prize,' she warbled, 'we have this beautiful wedding ring quilt by Mrs. Patterson.'

"Two of the girls in white paraded dramatically onto the stage, holding the quilt between them like they were about to fold a bed sheet.

"Mrs. Langhorne continued, plucking winners for the chocolate cream pies, the cinnamon rolls, the floral arrangements, and finally, the Zenith Stratosphere table-top radio.

"Then a hush fell upon the crowd, as if Mrs. Kelly, the librarian, had lifted a finger to her pursed lips.

"The Reverend's sister took over, and for this old Mrs. Langhorne was grateful. A fine sheen of sweat had collected at her forehead and she would have been mortified had anyone known that her silk shirt was stained under the arms, as if she were a common laborer. She returned to her seat in the front row.

"Old Dr. Brubaker's nurse in her pressed white dress and cap brought in the baby, wrapped in a snow-white blanket, a halo of curls around her head. The nurse placed the tiny bundle into the spinster's outstretched arms. Who could not see the ray of happiness on a face that would never see her own child?

"There was such a gasp from the audience that Mrs. Langhorne's old and sad heart sunk. Then there was silence. And then, such a scurry as you would not believe. Hats and gloves were collected, programs stuffed into handbags and pockets, and folks climbed over each other to leave their seats. Now, it wasn't the whole crowd, mind you, but more than half. The thing of it was, those people who had scraped together just enough money had come to see the show, old Mrs. Langhorne, and whatever nonsense the rich lady had cooked up. They had no intention of taking home a child. When they read the newspaper article, they had thought the story a ruse. A curiosity.

"At first, the five majorette baton twirlers who marched in the high school band did not know what to do. They had been enlisted —so fine in their red uniforms and smart berets—to guard the church entrance so the riff-raff from the hollers didn't try to sneak in. Imagine their surprise when they encountered a hoard of people trying to get out. A woman with a peacock feather in her hat pushed one of the majorettes aside roughly, and then all the girls shifted in one solid red wave.

"More than thirty raffle tickets were drawn before a winner rose from the audience. It belonged to a couple just passing through on their honeymoon. He said he was a Hollywood director who would do anything to please his wife. On a lark, he had purchased a ticket. And so, the baby, with its accompanying accoutrements, was swept out of Tennessee and on to California. No one knew if the baby had gone to a good Christian family after all.

"After the raffle, a quiet fell over the town like a blanket. There was nothing left to say. It was as if the town had abandoned itself after the horrifying misunderstanding.

"Now the next day was Sunday. And old Mrs. Langhorne dressed as she always did, with care and precision. But that morning a dread hung in her heart. The day ticked on and the Reverend did not come to give her communion. The callers she expected on her doorstep to laud and praise her for the success of the raffle did not appear. Finally, at eight in the evening, she had her girl put away all the tea things: the silver pot, the bottles of soda pop, the finger sandwiches, the cream puffs and cookies, the hard-boiled eggs, and the ham loaf. The girl was allowed to take some of the feast home to her own children. This was old Mrs. Langhorne's rare and last act of kindness, and this is how she was to meet her maker. That night in her sleep, she died, the shame of the raffle baby scandal too great to bear.

"If you go back to the town, you will find that no one will talk about that day. The newspaperman, who so prominently ran the story of the baby on the front page, did not print another article. The posters and placards came down. Old Mrs. Langhorne was buried quietly beside her husband, Jasper Jones Langhorne. Her gravestone read simply: 'Cecily Langhorne, beloved wife of JJL,' and the dates she was born and died."

Teeny finished her tale with a slight bow and the women gathered their raggedy children and headed into their tents. The men gravitated together to smoke and chew. Those who knew the ludicrous nature of Teeny's stories understood they were good only for a momentary escape. When her narratives were done, her words toppled back down to the ground, and the moment was crushed by gravity. Nouns and verbs were abandoned under foot. The bleakness of the world returned.

Teeny's were not the only stories in the jungle. One 'bo passed information on to another and then to another and so on, in the way of a domino game. See. One little push, and everyone falls down: one beside a track, another under the blow of a bull's bat. It was important to know which conductor would push a 'bo off a train, then go back to his coffee and biscuit. Our jungle neighbors told which brakeman, who rode the caboose, would let you sit in the locomotive, warming a while by the fire, and those for whom cruelty was as easy as bending a slice of bread into a sandwich.

'Boes knew which town would give you a meal and a bath, and which sheriff would pick his teeth and scratch his belly as he watched fifty 'boes file into a ten-by-ten jail cell.

Unlike Teeny's tales, the news of the road and rails was true. True like the words I've given you. True like the tears you may shed when I finish my story. Around the fire, a hobo's stories put flies in our mouths and centipedes in our ears.

One 'bo killed another over a bar of soap. Bulls in disguise would ride a boxcar, get to know you, then shoot you in the back. If there was a crime committed anywhere near a jungle, a hobo was sure to have committed it. Some towns burned a jungle to the ground as if it were a pile of fall leaves. A black hobo—guilty or innocent—could not find justice anywhere. Many people thought that any hobo who just wanted equal treatment was a red, so it didn't pay to talk politics.

The newspapers printed stories about hobo signs and slangs. Truly. So the common man would know what we were up to and could fell us before we could utter a word.

Oh, there were light-hearted happy 'boes, full of wine and sass, and they told us about the hobo king who visited the White House, and a hobo college in New York City. And there was a convention where thousands of hoboes came together for a hobo gathering.

But really, a sad lot of us were children. What did we want with conventions and kings and college mumbo-jumbo? We wanted to snare squirrels and steal tomatoes, find a comic book in a trash can, know that we were safe together.

Chapter Eleven

Did you ever guess that three years would pass and Vic, Teeny, and I would still be together? But see here. Three years for you and three years for us, well, let's say they are not one unto the other. Time had no consequence, back then. And come to think of it, not so much now, either, as I watch ninety years approach one hundred.

We had nowhere to go and nowhere to be beyond where we would find our next job. When we decided one morning to go this way or that, we always ended up in the same place—looking for food and a place to sleep.

I do not think you know time as I did then. In 1936, 1937 and 1938, our lives hung suspended. We were moving and aging and standing still, all at the same time. No, it's not like being in limbo. When we are in limbo, we are waiting to decide between one thing or another, or to have that decision made for us. Limbo is book-ended by a beginning and an end. For us there was only the endless middle.

We traveled a loop. Do you take the same route to work and home again? I bet you do. So, you know the grip of familiarity. As you travel past landmarks and tombstones, so we went to California or Georgia or Oregon.

We had to avoid the dust storms; there was no work in those states. We spent winters in Winter Haven, Florida, picking and packing citrus. We headed to California in the spring, going hundreds of miles north before turning west to pick the cornucopia in lush California valleys. We picked apples in Washington and Ohio. Peaches in Georgia. Blueberries in Maine. Way up north in Minnesota and North Dakota we harvested sugar beets in the Red River Valley. We rode and hitched and begged. And when we had to, we stole.

We learned all the best scams from Vic, but we only took from those who could afford to give. Teeny proved to be a remarkable actress. She did not seem to age or grow any bigger, and Vic and I always towered over her. Since she always looked like a little lost waif, we used trickery to get what we needed. Teeny would distract our mark at the front door while Vic and I entered a house through the back and raided the kitchen. Teeny would offer to work for a meal, and then would collapse in the front yard. This is when Vic and I would steal eggs and chickens from the back. It worked almost every time, until it became second nature. We did not need to speak as we entered a neighborhood. We just took our places, like pieces on a chess board.

After three long years on the road, we all became dark, in our own way. Vic's bright yellow Viking hair became dull with the dirt of the road and soot of the coal until he finally allowed Teeny to trim it until he was almost bald—the only way to get rid of the lice and fleas. His *Reader's Digest* had long run out of space in its tiny white margins. The book stayed in his pocket more than it came out. He knew its contents by heart, and there was no room for more. And truth be told, he did not have the heart to start anew, though he could have swiped another easy from a library.

And my darkness? It was more of an obsession. I thought I

could keep Teeny safe if I did not smile, so the shadows settled in upon me.

As the days passed and the endless road stretched out, Teeny's stories and songs became thunder and lightning. Her fairytales turned into the ghost stories that hinted at nightmares that were catching up with her.

She was like a library book, I recall thinking, going on its merry way, making tales and half-truths. Not knowing Teeny's truth made it difficult to understand her. I believe that is why we were so protective of her. We knew she wasn't a gypsy girl or a raffle baby or a rebellious nun. But that is all we knew, so we let her be the heroine in the stories she wrote for herself.

Returning to the same tomato farm in 1937, we ran into the same migrant families. Some of the same children crowded around Teeny, not as toddlers but as thin reeds who had grown inch upon inch until a few were taller than she. It appeared as if some even wore the same tattered clothes. Sleeves that once stopped at wrists didn't fall beyond elbows. Pants that once brushed ankles stopped at mid-calf. Toes stuck two inches out of the front of a shoe. Or no shoe at all.

While their fathers smoked and their mothers tidied, Teeny sang and told stories that made children turn away from her for the first time. She meant to give cookies and pies with her words, but instead she poured out vinegar.

She told the story of a lost girl who froze to death in the mountains of Tennessee. Before she died, the Lord himself had given her the choice of freezing or being devoured by bobcats. The sad little girl sat down against a tree trunk and took her fate. Teeny told the story of the poor crippled girl whose spiteful adopted parents sold her leg braces and made her work in a factory, sorting tiny pearl buttons twelve hours a day.

And when Teeny sang, the children buried their faces in their mothers' shoulders and wept, but Teeny sang on:

"A long time ago there were two little babes...they were left in the wood...they sobbed an' they sighed...they laid down and died...when they were dead...the little robins so red...brought strawberry leaves...an' over them spread...all the day long...they sang them this song...poor babes in the woods."

Teeny delivered one of her last fireside stories in a jungle of 'boes who didn't much care to hear it, but who had precious little else to do. So, while they rolled cigarettes and mended socks, they listened as Teeny spun yet another sad, sad tale.

"There was an orphan girl forced by an evil man to steal wallets and snatch purses. She wandered the streets of Nashville, like a little waif, in a dirty blue dress. Her golden curls unfurled behind her like ribbons. One day, the police took away the man, and from that point on, she would pick a pocket only when she needed to, and only from a man who carried a silver-tipped cane or wore a fashionable silk top hat. She did not steal from the poor. Why, that would be like stealing from herself!

"All day she dreamed of white unicorns, frilly dresses, teddy bears and other little girl things. She was a sweet little doll, even if she was a thief, and all she wanted was a family.

"Her hair shone in the sunlight, and when the rain poured down it looked like ropes of wet gold. Finely dressed women, especially, were drawn to the small child, and one day, she did not have to steal anymore.

"A lady wearing a silk dress the color of violets stopped the girl on the street and held an umbrella over her tiny body. When she learned that the girl had no mother and no father, the pretty lady stepped to the curb and put out her hand. Soon, a large black automobile stopped and a man in a fancy hat helped them into the back seat.

"The car drove the girl and the lady to a fashionable house on a pretty tree-lined street near the center of the city. It took up an entire block. When the girl climbed the steps with the lady, it seemed that an entire army came to greet them. A man in a serious suit opened the door and helped them inside. A big woman in an apron took the girl to the kitchen and made her sandwiches: thick slices of ham on fluffy white cloud bread. She drank lemonade in a real glass and watched as the big woman cut a wedge of chocolate cake and put it before her on a china plate so thin she was afraid it would break as soon as the fork touched it.

"Then a maid in a cap took the girl to an inside bathtub that gleamed in a white tile room. No sooner had the girl removed her clothes that they were whisked away by an unknown hand, and the girl climbed into water that smelled like roses. When the girl was dry, the pretty lady came in and brushed her golden hair, then took her to a little girl room with a pink frilly bed and white lacy curtains, where she helped her into a white dress with a sash the color of a buttercup. There once had been another little girl, just like her, the lady explained. And this had been her room until she went to be with the angels.

"The pretty lady wore red lipstick and silver stockings and took the little girl's hand and showed her around the house and garden. Outside, a swimming pool twinkled at them, and the pretty lady promised she would have a new swimsuit every summer. A bouncy white puppy chased squirrels around the lawn and barked when they ran up a tree. The lady led her back inside and up the stairs. She let the little girl sit on her white satin bed and watch as she made up her eyes, sprayed perfume on her neck, and slipped into a slinky black evening gown. Now dressed and gleaming, the woman kissed the girl on the cheek and took her back to the frilly pink room where she would sleep.

"'Good night, my darling,' the lady said to the girl. 'Tomorrow we will go for ice cream and buy you dresses and shoes. Would you like that?'

"The girl nodded, then the woman kissed her forehead, and the girl could smell roses again.

"The little girl was so happy. Too happy, really. She lay under the lacy white quilt in the pink room. And thinking of the chocolate cake and the puppy, and the only kindness she had ever known, she died, too happy to go on living."

You see why my mood is dark. Because Teeny's was.

But now, my mood is darker than when I began. Can you blame me? I have grown weary thinking of the sad stories Teeny told. And we are reaching the fork in the road, where each of us went our separate ways.

Each day, each week, each year was the same as the other. I have more stories to tell, but why? They are iterations of the ones I've already told you. They are the same gravel on the road you have already traveled with me.

You want to know, did she love me? You want to know if I ever held her hand or rested my work-worn palm on her lower back. These things existed in my mind, and somehow that was enough. I was her protector. I had her attention. She needed me. Was I a silly boy with a crush? You must decide for yourself. Remember at the beginning, when you held out your hands, and I said I would give you only the words you need? That is still true. I have given you the words, as I promised. But for some things, you'll have to paint a picture.

I never imagined there would be a time without her, for I never imagined life beyond my next meal. So when that time came, I was not prepared for what happened. It is so often the case. The most important moment of your life does not declare itself while it is approaching.

You must brace yourself for what is to come next.

We were on a hotshot in September of thirty-eight, headed north and east. Let me pause and remind you that any train with a fast route, priority freight, and few stops was a hotshot. It would get you from one part of the country to another, fast. We boarded in south Georgia, joining a crowded boxcar with thirty other 'boes.

We did not expect the train to stop for hours and hours, and sunk onto the floor to sleep, leaning against each other.

Do you ever wake in a start, perhaps in a strange hotel room or in a friend's guest room, and momentarily have no idea where you are? That night, we did, Teeny, Vic and I and the flock of 'boes who shared our rickety berth. The train screeched and coughed to a halt and then the doors flew open and we were blinded by lanterns, which revealed five heavy-set bulls, rifle butts resting on hips and pointed toward us with fingers on triggers.

"Round 'em up, Russ," one of them said. "Get the girls and the young ones."

The man called Russ emerged in front of the pack of bulls and started grabbing for the boys, hoisting them up by collars and waistbands and throwing them out of the car where I could hear other bulls herding them into cars and trucks.

"This is the end of the road, girls," the man said. "It's time you went home."

Vic and I moved to push Teeny behind us but the man called Russ was too quick. He smacked Vic in the head with the butt of his rifle, and before we knew it, Teeny was out of the boxcar.

I did not hesitate but threw myself at one of the bulls, knocking us both out of the box. All around me young 'boes, the smallest and saddest of them all, were being kicked and thrown out of the boxcars, spilling out like a bag of rice split open with a blade. In the silvery moonlight I saw that Teeny had gotten away from her captor, and she was making good time. I ran after her, dodging bullets. I fell in beside her and grabbed at her hand when I saw that she was about to stumble, but her tiny fingers slipped away. And as she tried to steady herself, one of her boots fell off, and she went down. In that instant, a bull appeared as if from nowhere, and grabbed her around the waist with a powerful arm, lifting her onto his shoulder. For she was that light. He held the rifle in the other hand, and it was pointed at me. I ran in a zigzag pattern and avoided his bullets. I heard her yell my name.

You know the saying about when the time of your death is upon you, you see your life flash before your eyes? Well, that is not so. You see the lives of others. Of a gypsy girl, of a baby held by do-gooders on a stage, of a little girl frozen to the ground. Teeny's stories crowded in my mind.

"Teeny," I yelled, circling back despite the gun that was determined to stop me.

"My name is Homer Giles!" I yelled, over and over, for she only knew me as Sonny Boy.

"Homer Giles Homer Giles I love you I love you." For those words had become my name, too. "Homer Giles Homer Giles I come from Connellsville outside Pittsburgh. Connellsville Homer Giles I love you I love you outside Pittsburgh."

The bull shoved her into a police wagon, one of six or seven waiting like tanks along a desolate stretch of land that could have been anywhere, anyplace. Ohio. Carolina. Tennessee. Illinois. She kicked and bit, her feet banged on the wagon as he shoved her in. The bull's hat fell to the ground and the wind blew his tightly wound sandy waves into a storm. I came upon him them, hopped onto his back, and pulled those waves, taking handfuls of tufts from the scalp. But he shoved me away, then slipped into the driver's seat and sped away. The van was full, you see, and there was no room for me. Only room for a tiny girl. I ran after the car, yelling my name. But it was no use.

I felt a kick in my back and fell to the ground. A bull kicked again while another one wrestled me up and drug me back onto the boxcar. The train had started its evil departure.

Two bulls remained on the car with us, eyes hard, rifles pointed toward us. We shouted and protested and insisted that they tell us where we were. Fathers wanted to know where they had lost their sons you see, just as I needed to know where I had lost Teeny. But the bulls just laughed and kicked sawdust in our faces. Wherever they were taking us, once we arrived nothing good would greet us.

Before the bulls had closed the doors, I looked up at the light blue water tower hovering over us. In the silvery light, I saw a cartoon-like Dutch man and woman in exaggerated red wooden shoes painted on one side. The woman's pigtails stuck out from either side of her head, and glossy yellow ribbons framed her face. The man wore denim coveralls with only one strap. I let the heat of the July night wash over me. I would never forget this day. This ordinary Tuesday when everything changed.

The bull carrying the lantern slammed the door shut, narrowly missing my nose, and laughed at the near miss. I watched him worry the toothpick from one side of his mouth to the other. His shirt strained across a belly full of Sunday roasts, apple pies, bacon and eggs. He smelled of onions and garlic—food that we would have killed for.

I held my sleeve to Vic's bleeding forehead. A small line of blood trickled down his check and dropped onto his collar. I was reminded of the old cow drinking our glasses of lemonade, a small yellow stream of liquid drizzling out of her mouth, down her chin and onto her dress. I pressed my sleeve harder against Vic's head to stem the bleeding. He did not lose consciousness. His eyes were open, but I knew that somewhere deep inside, he slept, battered and torn. My eyes were open too, seeing all the injustices that had been done to us. For so long they seemed to be few and far between, something that we could handle now and again. But this was too much. I feared it would break us. It had broken Teeny.

Surely you have heard the old proverb: "For want of a nail." It means that nothing is *just* anything. A nail neglected can be the downfall of civilization. A hand-me-down pair of boots can make a girl disappear.

And that is just what happened. We never replaced Teeny's too-big boots, you see. And for want of a boot, my friend was lost.

Teeny always said of her boots, "They're all right boys, just like you. Rough around the edges, but the sole's real swell." Or she'd say, "We've been a pair this long, it'd be a shame to split us up." She loved to play with words that way and tinkled with laughter at her own silly jokes. And it amused Vic to appease her, so we let it go.

When Vic coughed up a dime for a treat she would buy shoelaces and a pot of polish. She kept up those boots like she was going to church. The laces were the preacher. The shine was the choir.

It wasn't until I had my own daughter, with her flights of fancy and ill-fated choices, that I understood I should have insisted on new boots for Teeny. I wondered sometimes why those beat-up old boots were so important to her, and wished that, all those times in the jungles when I watched her patch and mend them, I had asked her. Perhaps if the boots had been red, like her fiery hair or painted nails, they would have bestowed a magical power to protect her. Perhaps not.

Hours into our ride, the throng of 'boes rushed the bulls, knocking them and the rifles to the floor. They kicked and kicked until the men were still, though their groans signaled they were still alive. Two boes stripped the men, as if tearing off a deer hide with one deft slash of a knife. Bounty secured, an old man 'bo, called Reed because of his tall, stark frame, slid open the box door with a grin. A few others grabbed the bulls and threw them into the passing night. The train was speeding like a hotshot always does, seventy or so miles an hour. We heard the two thumps, one after another, as the fall spun the bodies under the wheels. The 'boes cheered and laughed and shared smokes, when ordinarily they would not have been so generous. The pickings were divided up, though there was not enough for all. The smaller men, whose eyes sunk into grey faces, sat meekly away from the fray. Nobody noticed Vic and me in the corner. We looked at each other. We were unfazed by the violence. Yes, it was terrible. But we did not care. Not then. If we had seen this any other time, we would have reacted differently. But that day was a sweater turned inside out.

The train chugged on for hours and hours. We were going further and further away from Teeny, but it hardly mattered. For we did not know where we were when she had been taken. In the three years we had been traveling together, we had only been separated twice. The first was when Teeny stayed with the farmer in Iowa and we went to Oregon to pick peas. The next time, we had been camping in a field in late July, when a farmer came out of nowhere with a shotgun and started firing. Teeny managed to get away but he held Vic and me in place with his gun, and the next day made us work for hours in his sweet potato field, pulling weeds, row after endless row. When he bored of watching us he wandered away. Not knowing where Teeny was, we had no choice but to stay until she returned, which she did, the following day, carrying a sack of fried chicken, lemon squares and apples. Vic decided then that if we were ever separated, we would return in two days' time to the place where we were last together. We began to call this our "third day," and hoped it never arrived. But, of course, this time, we had no idea where to return. And now that we needed it, there could be no third day. Oh, how often that painful irony would haunt me.

The train stopped in the Chicago yards and Vic and I walked and thumbed our way west toward Davenport, where we would find plenty of jungles along the Mississippi. That mighty river was a watery train, chugging its way from Minnesota up north all the way down to New Orleans. We spread the word about Teeny as we went, and many 'boes and migrant families remembered her, and promised to say we were looking for her should they see her.

But what of it, you wonder? What good did it do to tell a girl that we were looking for her, when she wouldn't know how to find us? Vic and I took comfort in the notion that all girls were sent home, though what we thought but did not speak aloud was we didn't know what kind of home she had. For neither of us believed she was the gypsy girl who travelled with Magda, her quasi-foster mother.

Sometimes I told myself that Teeny had escaped the bulls after all and had fled to Grandfather Mountain. But I would not let myself take that thread of thought further, so as not to start to think that she was waiting for me there. Vic and I did not speak of Teeny again. He was practical—I told you he was north—and believed that Teeny had been rescued, rather than stolen. Stolen was south, you see, and we were always headed north.

Chapter Twelve

Friend. You have been with me for a while. And I thank you. But I can no longer hold my tongue. For I have lied to you. I told you before that when I helped Vic punish Roley, that was my only act of violence. It is not so. It was, however, my only willing act of violence. I was too scared to speak of this before. Forgive me for what I am about to tell you. Please stay with me until the end of my tale, despite what you are about to learn. For now, you are as much a part of this story as I am. And I need you.

Not long after we lost Teeny, with Davenport come and gone, Vic and I decided to head toward California. Without Teeny, we took more chances than ever, and decided to ride through Kansas, right through the worst of the dirt storms.

We hopped into a box on the Missouri Pacific, relieved that the conductor had been a good sort and not booted us off. Soon I understood why. It was our bad luck the train got stuck on tracks in western Kansas when it ran into a dust mountain, on the heels of a big boy of a windstorm. The conductor stopped and put all us 'boes to work. With shovels, tin cups, and even our hands, we moved the dust drifts from the tracks.

It was the first time either Vic or I had felt the dust. Oh, we had tasted Oklahoma, Texas, and parts of Kansas, as their soil defied gravity and deposited a thin film of dust in its wake, even back in the East. And we had heard stories of the billowing dark clouds and the gas masks people wore. But in our hands, the dust doubled as the inhumanity we seemed always to be dodging.

After our work was done, we scrambled up the catwalks ready to hear the thrust of the steam and the rocking of the cars. But instead, the conductor powered down at the sound of a whining siren, announcing the arrival of bulls. For our hard labor, the bulls rewarded us with a kick or a slap atop our heads. But instead of taking us to jail, bulls and deputies handed each of us—at least one hundred—a club or stick and herded us for a mile or so toward a gathering crowd.

For as far as I could see, across the dead, windswept land, jackrabbits ran this way and that, their ears made larger by their emaciated bodies, their eyes protruding like sores. There were thousands of them. Some stopped to sniff the ground looking for grass. Others hopped on or over each other. This was the frenzy of something that had gone very wrong.

Someone had erected hasty wire fencing into a makeshift enclosure stretching for what seemed like miles. The crowd stood in rows forming a square and began to move in as one, herding the rabbits into the middle of the enclosure. Men and boys wielded clubs, like ours. Behind them, women and girls honked car horns and banged pots and wooden spoons. Soon, Vic and I and all the other 'boes were swept into the surge. We stood, shoulders touching, inching forward. There was nowhere for the rabbits to go, except into the enclosure.

The people of Morris Township, Kansas, had turned out in their Sunday best that day, though nothing was white anymore. Not collars or ladies' gloves or dresses. Even skin, wind-burned and rough, was not white. Everywhere—under fingernails, between teeth, in very pores—tiny grains of sand wedged themselves, singing the song of the stubborn caraway seed.

Traveling as we did, we were unaccustomed to very large groups of people clustered together, shoulder-to-shoulder, ear to ear. Even in the fields, where we picked among the strangers who became our constant companions for a stretch of time, we never touched. And we were unaccustomed to seeing decent folks welcome us with cheers and shouts. The gathered crowds that day did not turn away from us in disgust or pity. The women did not gather their children close as we shuffled past. Instead, they welcomed us. Players in their horrible game.

And so, it was beginning.

See here. Do not go to the internet to find out more. You will not like what you see.

I will never forget the sound a club makes when it cracks the skull of a rabbit, then another, and another. Like a call and response song. Crack. Then a shriek from the poor creature. Then, thud. The sound of one rabbit corpse hitting another on a growing pile.

Crack. Shriek. Thud.

Crack. Shriek. Thud.

We clubbed rabbits of all sizes, once content together in their underground mazes. Mothers. Daughters. Sons. Children. Fathers. Struck down in a murderous frenzy so cruel that only fear and desperation could be responsible.

That crowd of hundreds killed more than eight thousand rabbits that afternoon. I know because the sheriff made a tally. And when the last rabbit was tossed onto the pile, the crowd cheered at the proclamation. A newspaperman took a photo of the pile of bodies, the sheriff and the mayor standing proudly beside the pitiful mass.

You will want to know my part in this cruel practice. At first, I did not move my club. I clenched it to my side. Vic did, too. I hunched into myself, trying to fold my body in half like a piece of paper disappearing into an envelope. But the sheriff's deputies were having none of it, and they punched and shoved us until they saw that we had lifted our arms. I tried to move the club like a feather and land it on the ground like a pillow. But a deputy punched my gut. Another kicked my shin. I tried to miss when I swung my arm down. But there were so many of them. Thousands stampeded over each other in a futile attempt to escape the brutality. Our lives were intertwined for one long and gruesome hour. They were fated to die, and I was forced to kill them.

For among the people of Morris Township, each smack of a club was a retaliation against the betraying soil. A raised arm was a fist raised against a tractor that had nothing to do, and a well that had nothing to give.

After the rabbit drive, the sheriff congratulated us and rewarded each 'bo with two rabbits. Neither Vic nor I could bring ourselves to grab the creatures from the pile. Some were still alive, making pitiful mewling and whimpering sounds. No one was willing to waste a bullet on a goddamned jackrabbit.

And as despicable as this practice was, I could not blame the people of Morris Township.

No, don't judge me just yet. First, hear me. You were not there. You did not see. For a decade, the dust storms brought night into day, swept away the people's livelihood, suffocated their starving cattle until they succumbed, and killed their children with black pneumonia. And then, a plague of rabbits came and consumed all they had left. Any remnants of a sorry, stringy excuse for a vegetable garden still growing, was gone in the blink of an eye. The rabbits were starving, and they descended together in Biblical proportions on people already beaten down by bankers and dirt.

After the rabbit drive, the deputies marched us back to the train and handed us shovels. We resumed our digging, but before we were done, the wind sent us chasing after our caps and scrambling into boxcars. Even though the doors were closed, the dust collected in corners like snow drifts, and speckled our skin.

Later that night, the howling wind the very echo of the deadly dust, I heard Vic climb out of the boxcar. I tiptoed quietly behind him and hung back so he wouldn't see me. He disappeared behind a thicket of tumbleweed, the only crop to survive in that wretched land. Presently, he began to sob, and his bright Viking hair bobbed up and down like the yellow petals of dandelions.

I will pause here to tell you more of Vic. He has been a whisper in this tale so far. I must amplify him.

What do you know so far? Let me pull it together for you here. He was a tall and strapping Viking man-child, with yellow hair that served as a beacon in a crowd. You have seen his heart in a dollar bill, in a half-portion of beans, in a private sob. Like me, he was of few words on the road, and he had told me the story of his foster childhood in the time it took to consume a meagre meal of stolen bread.

Have you wondered why I, and then Teeny, followed him almost blindly? Do you think less of me because I let him lead me? Please don't. I was smart enough to know that I needed Vic, that we needed Vic. We were always one step behind him and he was always ten or so paces into what came next. And while he rarely shared his plan with us, we knew he would deliver us to safety, for he had the compass, at least for a time: the worn *Reader's Digest* magazine with his sacred scribbles in the margins. His notes were the New Testament. His symbols, the Proverbs. Before he took us in, he had crossed the country I don't know how many times. When he opened his eyes in the mornings he saw the grid of railroad tracks stretching from one coast to the other. For six years, he had studied those around him. He had learned to read a person. A train. A place. He knew when to tip his cap and when to turn on his heel. And we learned to read him. He had a grunt of satisfaction, and another that told us to slow down, to think twice. He could tell us to stop whining with the tilt of his chin, and to watch out, by cocking his head and stretching his neck. Teeny knew all these indicators, too, but she ignored them. Vic had a special eye roll for me to tell me to "Get that girl in line, Sonny Boy."

Vic delivered us into the kind of safety you would scoff at. And here in my old age, I might too. In a week, if we had ten of twenty-one meals, we had Vic to thank. Now, don't blame Vic for the rabbit drive or the old cow who cheated us. Don't blame him for Roley.

What was Vic's crowning achievement in his life? I can only tell you his crowning achievement in mine: he kept me from freezing in the winter. That is no small accomplishment for a pair of beggars and thieves who kept a tiny girl under their wings.

That first winter, when all was new in our trio and we inched toward Florida for the citrus harvest, I understood why Vic had misered away our earnings. Have you been to the upper Midwest in January? Hear tell from Vic, the winter of 1935-1936 was the coldest on record. I didn't know it then, but Georgia Joe had lost the top half of his ears to frostbite that year. That's why he was never without his porkpie hat, Vic told us.

The winter of 1936-1937, we stumbled across the plains in a connect-the-dots fashion. Sometimes we paid to ride a train or a bus. We hitched and walked only when we had to. At night, Vic found a down-and-out hotel and we stayed the night for fifty cents. More if we wanted a bath, or if the desk clerk noticed Teeny before we snuck her in. It was better if we came upon a roadside motel, for the rooms were apart from the office and it was easy to usher Teeny in after dark. You do not want to know what we heard and saw while in those rooms, and every time we crossed the threshold I hated the fact that we had nothing better to give Teeny.

She was content, but only as a child is content while occupied with a pastime. She would take the bed and we would sleep on the floor. She would scrub her hands clean and take Vic's pocketknife under her nails. She would polish her boots, admire herself in the cracked compact, and paint her fingers with the red polish Vic grudgingly allowed her to buy.

Sometimes we could rent a room in an old lady's house, and she might provide a hot breakfast and then wipe her eyes with her apron because she could not give us more than coffee, toast, and porridge. If we were desperate, we stopped in abandoned warehouses tucked away in an urban no-man's-land, where only the darkest and meanest 'boes dared go. Vic did not sleep those nights. He knew that any one of the drifters would slit our throats for a go at our shoes.

We did not come out of that first winter unscathed. Don't think that for one minute. Bronchitis settled in Teeny's chest, and we lingered for two weeks in a boarding house, watching the coins pass from Vic into the landlord's hand. And more went to a doctor who came with a pot of vapor rub and half bottle of cough syrup he swore was new.

We learned in Iowa later that spring that Blue had slipped on an icy catwalk, falling to his death beneath the wheels, and Mutt was last seen with an old buzzard, leading him away, his arm around his shoulders possessively. Bo Wrinkles was still alive. Funny, I thought then, how that feeble old man was still hanging on.

Ho! You are thinking the same about me. But don't you want me to keep going? Surely you are pleased that I am still here, for you want to hear the end of the story, do you not?

If I could see Vic now, I would not have the words to thank him. Over the years, I sometimes looked for his Viking yellow hair in crowds, before I knew that I was doing so. It might be that when I opened a newspaper on a lazy Sunday morning I would wonder fleetingly if I might see him in the financial section, or in the list of declared politicians. For that is how highly I thought of him. He was Henry Ford. Edison. Rockefeller.

Vic left me after the jackrabbits. The rails and the thumb had worn him down to a human nub. He was eighteen by then and could go to the Triple C's. (That's Civilian Conservation Corps to you, or CCC.) President Roosevelt had created an alphabet of jobs to feed and clothe a raggedy nation. Vic begged me to go with him to Utah where he would build roads and plant trees for Uncle Sam, sleep in a warm bunk and eat three meals a day. Beyond that, he did not care what lay ahead. I could find work cutting lumber near the CCC camp. He'd bring me food when he could, he said. I learned then that Vic had been following the progress of the CCC in all those visits to the libraries. Turns out, it didn't even bother him that part of his CCC paycheck would go to the foster father who took a strap to him. Vic just wanted something else. I couldn't blame him. His shoes, and his heart, were more worn out than my own.

Going with Vic felt like leaving Teeny, though I had no idea where she was or where we'd lost her. It felt to me that *I* had lost her.

That day in 1938, I watched as Vic walked into town. His shoulders were no longer hunched. He was a working man now. Later, when I picked up my pack to hit the road, I saw the worn *Reader's Digest* and a one-dollar bill waiting for me, like talismans.

Chapter Thirteen

W ithout Teeny and Vic to anchor me, I slipped under the surface of my own life, and alone with my thoughts, I became half mad with grief and anger. I felt I had betrayed her. I had not insisted on better fitting shoes. I had not stood in front of her like a human shield. I did not break the window or jump on the hood of the van that carried her away. There was so much I hadn't done.

And so, all that remained was for me to play the scene over and over again in my mind. It was like taking a fork and picking out my brains. Sometimes, I rewrote the ending. I imagined myself getting to Teeny in time, picking up her boot in one hand while throwing her over my shoulder with my other. I inserted a crowd of 'boes, bunched together, into my replay, and I ran through them, like I would a wheat field, and so escaped from the bulls. Sometimes I imagined that we had not even been on that train at all. But like Teeny's stories, when the words of my imaginings were done, all that remained was reality, bitter on my tongue.

I left Kansas and lost myself in the work that gradually became more available as the economy began to show signs of an upturn, albeit a slow one. Along the Missouri, I loaded barges and fixed ropes. On a gambling boat, I washed dishes for a week before moving northeast into Iowa. I skittered from one small northern town to another, like a game of cat's cradle—Mason City, Decorah, Cresco, Estherville.

I took to the libraries, as if spurred by the power of the memories of our phantom trio. I washed and tidied as best I could, as Teeny would have wanted. In the still, silent reading rooms, I devoured Vic's newspapers alongside other 'boes, who were not as particular about their hygiene. I read Teeny's women's magazines, once again imagining the domestic bliss that was more pretend than promise. I read recipes for hamburger casserole, chicken à la king, and Waldorf salads made with slivers of apples the size of a child's thumbnail. I memorized the ingredients and instructions, losing myself in the promise of pre-heated ovens and fast-setting gelatins.

In Vic's newspapers, I read about the latest hobo parties, but I had not the heart for them anymore. What fun would they be without a tiny girl bustling with the bravado of a peacock? And I lacked the confidence that she provided. In truth, I found that there was much I could not do without Teeny by my side. All those years I had thought it was she who needed me. Funny thing, though. It was I who needed her.

While the other 'boes received the ill wind of a librarian's withering gaze, I was applauded for my interest and aptitude in current affairs. (Though I will admit that my interest in the ladies' magazines drew their puzzled gazes.) The old spinsters particularly took pity on me. They gave me deviled eggs and sweet pickles from their lunch baskets. And on many occasions, I might earn a coin for odd jobs and errands.

In the little town of West Branch, the librarian was a lonely slip of a woman who fairly shrank behind the reference desk of her one-room domain. A week passed before she brought out the fresh milk from her family's farm. She shared cheeses and venison sausages. We ate from her smorgasbord, perched on the back steps overlooking a stream. She told me of President Herbert Hoover and shared tales of his childhood, for I had somehow ended up in his birthplace. She regaled his exploits in the gem mines of far-flung China, where he was known as the man who could see through rocks to the treasures below. But when I spoke of the Big Trouble and the Hoovervilles I had seen on my travels, she went silent, and there was no more farm milk. No more cheeses or sausages. And so, I was on my way again, my worn and patched satchel slung over my shoulder, my belly full and a laugh on my lips. For what could I do but smile at the absurdity of a silly, unde-served grudge?

Those weeks of my connect-the-dots travel across Iowa, I learned that there are predators everywhere, not just in the jungle and not just in the guise of a dirty old buzzard.

My library adventures continued in Sioux City, a city tucked away at the very edge of the state. After a week, I rose above the fray of 'boes that scratched and smelled and was given the job of shelving books. Opal Mae, the very prim librarian of sixty or so, took a shine to me, though I could not abide the squeak of her corrective oxfords on the waxed floor, or the smell of garlic upon her breath. But she gave me dimes and apples from her brother's orchard, so I smiled, and in her company breathed only through my mouth. Presently, she showed me the small broom closet where she had fitted up a cot, blanket, and pillow. I could sleep there, she said. She would hide me right before closing time and let me out an hour before the library opened. It was a risky and unconven-tional plan, but as it was October and the nights were chilly. I gratefully accepted her unexpected, grandmotherly kindness.

You know already what I had not yet learned. Predators know not gender. After a week of tucking myself into bed each evening, Opal Mae appeared in the broom closet one night, waking me from a deep sleep. As I stumbled awake, my brain trying to catch up with the light that had awakened me, she stripped out of her dress and stood above me in her girdle and knickers. Her chest was bare and drooped like deflated balloons down to the nether regions. The ice blue veins along her stick-like arms traced a journey I did not want to take. I protested, but she climbed into bed with me anyway, and pinning me down, rubbed herself against me until she was satisfied. She fled then, dress in hand. She had not said a word. I lay dazed in my cot until I realized she had not locked the library door. I waited until dawn, collected my things, and hurriedly left Sioux City and old Opal Mae behind me.

I ventured south from there, sleeping under newspapers and cardboard in jungles along the way. I shared my meager coffers and accepted the company of worn-down men who sometimes could still offer a kind word. I was not afraid now. I believe you wear your experience, like a coat and hat. But I preferred my own company and kept to myself. When I found an abandoned rail yard, save for a few phantom boxcars that sat rotting like long-ago tombstones, I took refuge and outfitted a car for my needs. I found a pail and made a fire by day to dry my clothes and rotting feet. It was my own private jungle, and for a time, it was good. But after days of drinking from a nearby stream, I quickly realized that a contamination had gripped hold of my head and my bowels.

Fevered and confused though I was, I knew if I was to live, I had to find help. Somehow, I walked, more like stumbled, down the dusty dirt roads and occasional blacktops, until I came to another train yard. A kindly brakeman pulled me aboard, fed me, and let me sleep until the next stop. Then a traveling salesman took pity on me and drove me a few hours in the direction of Des Moines. When we were almost to the city, he dumped me unceremoniously at the last driveway he saw just before the turn that would take him to the city proper. Having completed his task, he turned toward Des Moines, certainly without another thought of me.

Whatever might be at the other end of that driveway, it seemed to my delirious mind to be as far away as the ocean. Even a desert mirage. But on I went. When the woman of the farmhouse (I will tell you here, for ease of understanding, her name was Murlona Zug) opened the door and ushered me in, I promptly tipped over and crashed onto her linoleum floor like a tree felled.

When I awoke, it was in a fresh-smelling bed with Murlona washing my face with a cool cloth. My eyes went to her face and then to the bowl of black water balanced on her lap. In that moment, I knew that she had pulled me back from a precipice. She smiled and told me to hush and to rest. I watched a dark gold cross dangle from her neck. It was the same color as her eyes.

Let me pause and give you here what you need to know before I continue. Murlona and her husband Early had lost their son the summer before. I saw it in Murlona's face before she told me. We shared a grief that occupied the same time and space.

With time and nourishment I grew strong again, and fully entered Murlona and Early's life. They slid me into their son's life like a belt through loops. I sat at Ben's place at the kitchen table, where his fingers once fiddled with the Formica top and made it curl. I slept under his football pennants. I even wore his clothes for a time. Lying in bed at night I could still feel the hard planks of a boxcar and see a bull charging along the tracks.

Gradually, I let the kindness of this couple wash over me. Theirs was a kindness so strong, it could kill the old cow who teased us with a dinner she never intended to feed us. It took away the grime around my neck. Kindness made my hair grow and strengthened my body. But it would not take away memory. Not just then.

The first week after they brought me into their home, I emerged from the fugue and fever to see that I was surrounded by the trimmings of an inside life. It was a world turned upside down. What once I mostly saw outside—a shaving mirror, a place to sleep, a can of beans—were now inside, like pieces in a museum.

My comfortable inside bed was like a slap in Teeny's face. How could it not be? My only consolation was what I eventually talked myself into believing: girl hoboes were not put in jail. They were sent home. Surely, buried somewhere in her fanciful tales, Teeny had a home.

At the beginning of my time with the Zugs the farm was a foreign land, for it had no trains. No signals or signs to lead the way. No jungles. But I had done much farm work in three years on the road, and soon I returned to the familiar rhythm of the farming year.

The farm's order and predictability were a balm to my aches. Someone once said that home is not a place, but a feeling. This was not true in my case. Home was very much the structure that literarily housed me. Early and Murlona's farm was much like the ones I had seen across the Midwest. In 1938, it was one of the few with electricity, and what a treat that was for me.

You might think that after so many days upon days on the road that I would feel boxed in by the confines of a house. But that was not the case. I relished defined boundaries. I loved the margins that bordered my life, like the instructions Vic kept in the margins of his worn *Reader's Digest* magazine. Confines predict. A boundary tells you what to do and where to go. It implies purpose and destination, and I followed it, as I had followed Vic.

That November, I followed the flagstone walk to get from the house to the wood shop. From there, I walked along a tree line to the barn. Every step I took from that day forward was precise. My feet knew where they were going, down to the grain of sand that would inhabit the bottom of my shoe. Out buildings still dotted the landscape, and I often retreated to the old smokehouse and abandoned icehouse for solace—a solace I longed for less and less.

Deciding what room or place to enter is like deciding what clothes to wear in the morning. At first, I sought only those smaller spaces on the periphery of the farm, disappearing for hours. Murlona and Early never asked where I went. I suspected they knew, though we never spoke of my time on the road. Oh, they knew I had not just simply come over from my home to theirs.

They just did not know what had happened before. In time, I spent more time with them inside.

Each room is a person. Each wall a blanket. Each floor a pillow. We spent our free hours in the family room. Surrounded by books and magazines, knitting and mending baskets, needlepoint pillows, doilies on armchairs, we froze that room in time. And it remained the same for the next five decades. My daughter read picture books on the same rag rugs Murlona beat on the clothesline every week. Eventually, I would take over Early's chair, being sure to carefully rub olive oil over cracks in the leather that spread out like the tributaries of the Mississippi. But that was years and years away. In those early weeks with the Zugs, I forced myself to accept that Teeny was a room I would not enter again. It doesn't matter if a room has a door or window, for if you don't know where it is or how to find it, there is no way in.

That first fall, Murlona lifted me up and buoyed my broken spirit with clean towels that smelled of pine and homemade soap specked with coffee grounds. She applied her sweet words like band-aids.

"Bless your heart."

"Angel."

"Sweet Pea."

On those early Saturdays, I stood alongside Murlona in her warm kitchen and together we prepared the recipes I had memorized from the ladies' magazines. I delivered lists of ingredients and paragraphs of cooking instructions like special trinkets one might put in a Christmas stocking. I wanted so much to give something to the woman who had taken me in. As we dredged chicken breasts in flour and paprika or cut into green peppers to make space for a tomatoey beef and rice filling, I basked in the curious glances she gave me. You see, sometimes the unexpected is the best gift of all.

Early was an accountant at the Iowa State Commerce Commission, but on his family's farm he raised cattle, selling a select portion every year. Doing farm chores side-by-side with Early gave meaning to my mornings. He was a hard, steady worker—the kind of man it's always good to be close to. And the farm felt good under my touch. The cow hide was rough upon my face. The eggs smooth in my hands. The dried hay yielded under my shoes. I saw a brilliant tapestry where none had been before.

What does a boy of fifteen do with a heart he cannot reveal is broken? Not because he doesn't want to, but because he just doesn't know how to. Anxiety thrummed through me when I thought of Teeny, her head bent over her shoe polish pot, or her eyes studying her red-tipped fingers.

I mourned Teeny in the only way my fifteen-year-old self knew how, for it was how Vic had mourned the rabbits. I am certain that I resembled him when I hid myself away somewhere on the farm, and let the silent sobs wrack my body. There was nothing else I could do, you see.

I saw her everywhere. A person can appear in a sliver of silvery moonlight or in a shoeshine kit, as she did for me whenever I buffed a pair of loafers or cleaned my suede two-tones with a small wire brush. I am sure you see by now that you can't get where you need to go if you don't have the right shoes.

Those first weeks, I carried my new life in buckets, careful to only spill it bit by bit, drop by drop, as if saving it as much as I could. Saving it to make sure it never ran out. And I would come to love Early and Murlona. Love them with hands I put to work on their farm. With the family I gave them.

Chapter Fourteen

But first.

There were hushed words spoken behind closed doors. There were Murlona's lingering looks and the creases on Early's forehead that said he had still not decided what to do with me.

Eventually, there were church services and sweet hymns on Sundays. Then trips to the feed store with Early. And family meals at the drugstore lunch counter.

And then, school.

This word, *school*, once spoken in Murlona's kitchen, was like a long awkward pause. A staring contest. A gunslingers' standoff.

I had not considered this, so long had it been since I had taken a pencil to math or re-inked my pen. I could not remember the last time I had looped letters onto cheap rag paper. Or raised my hand to answer a question. Or stood to pledge my allegiance.

Happiness came for me then like a springtime bloom, though it was winter. For I knew school meant I was to stay. Early concocted a story that I was his nephew from Virginia, having come to live with them after my parents' death. And that was that. No one questioned this story. Why would they? Murlona and

Early were churchgoers. Murlona crocheted shawls for the church's shut-ins. Early helped with their tax returns. This kind of people did not lie. They were the Michelin Man and Betty Crocker of their small Iowa town.

One morning, Murlona bundled me up in coats and blankets to drive us to the high school, for Ben's heater never did work quite right, she told me. Funny, sitting in Ben's dark blue Ford pick-up, wearing his clothes, loving his parents, I felt for the first time that I was me. So, you see, I wore Ben's happiness along with his clothes. At first, yes, it did seem surreal. Like one of Teeny's fairytales. Like I was a wicked twin or living in a parallel universe.

But the things that co-exist in our lives are the things that make it sweet. Ben's clothes covered my past, and so my present and future were born. It was his paper I rolled into his typewriter to write essays and themes. But my words came out, not Ben's. I knew I did not replace Ben, for he was very much alive, in the photos around the house, in the stories Murlona told. And that was fine. It was just as it should have been.

On my first day of school a boy named Fred introduced himself with a playful fist on my shoulder, and quickly he and his gang absorbed me into their orbit. I was swell and mysterious, coming all the way out to Iowa from the East. They had all known Ben. Admired him for his flashy smile, quick wit, and dapper argyle socks.

How should I describe my classmates? Now listen. At first, I did not have the words that defined them, for I had not spoken them in such a long time. But slowly they emerged: carefree, soft, naive, trustworthy, fun, happy.

At first, I did not know what I would do with my new friends, for their friendship was so unlike the friendships I had forged with Teeny and Vic during the three previous years. I especially did not know what to do with the girls. Their sparkling eyes, matching sweater sets and sprayed hair reminded me of shiny new toys. I could not help but stare. Sure, I had seen girls like them many times, across the road, in a restaurant window, walking a dog. But proximity makes a thing real. Those girls on the road were like a Greek chorus, or even paper dolls, who would never speak to me. Why, sometimes mothers and fathers on the sidewalk ahead would take their children by the elbow when they saw us 'boes coming and steer them across the street.

You may be surprised how quickly I assimilated. A crew cut, fresh clothes, even a splash of cologne, and I was taken from one extreme to another, as if there had been nothing in-between the two. The schedule of school and farm chores, of church on Sunday and dates on Saturday night, were like the boundaries of Early and Murlona's farm. I always knew where I was supposed to be, and how I relished this normal. I needed my new life as antidote against the ache of memory, just as Teeny had protected herself with shoelaces and fingernail polish.

In the first year with Murlona and Early, a scaffolding of sorts protected my fragile life, until I was ready to stand on my own. No, not the steel posts and ladders bordering an emerging skyscraper. My scaffolding protected me and elevated me with saddle shoes, a dance band or two, wool vests without holes, a ham cooked with cloves and brown sugar. I knew, even before the scaffolding came down, that I wanted my world always to be orderly and small. I would keep it close, where I could always see it.

I am not bragging, but you should know that I excelled, despite my three-year absence from my primary education. In the evenings, Early and Murlona sat at the Formica table and walked me through geometry, history, science, and literature. We rode the globe together, buoyed by Murlona's sweet tea, which we drank all year long as if it were medicinal. I suppose, for me at least, it was.

Murlona took me into Des Moines and the downtown department store. We bought new trousers, shirts, sweaters and shoes, unmentionables, socks, a winter coat, and hat. Even a suit to wear to all the dances she promised me I would attend. Murlona had seen my future in her mind and felt she must fill it with the necessary trappings.

After we shopped, she took me to the tearoom on the top floor and showed me how to hold a knife and fork, drink from a china cup, and arrange my cutlery on my plate when I was done eating.

Can you see me in a tearoom? No, I suppose you can't, for all this while you have seen mostly Vic, with his Viking stance and yellow hair, and Teeny, with her small bones and red nail polish.

So, I will show you now. You already know that I was tall for my age at twelve. By the time I sat in that tearoom—my big feet fighting with the lace tablecloth—I was six feet four inches. I had grown seven inches on the road. I did not know this until I saw a doctor for my first physical, and the nurse measured me. My dark cow licked hair, once so unruly despite Teeny's attempt at taming it, was now in a neat buzz cut. I never grew tired of running my palm against the flat top, feeling the bristles tickle me. My height prompted one leg to cross another and stretch out in front of me. Even if I had wanted to render myself small by stooping my shoulders or hunching my back, it would have made no difference. You cannot hide a bull in a field of goats.

That evening, while Murlona was putting away my new clothes, Early told me the story of our beginning together.

"When you stumbled into our kitchen, it was as if the Lord himself, or an angel, had deposited you here," he said. "Murlona had just finished telling me that she did not believe in God anymore. She insisted that no God of hers would take away her boy and cause her so much pain. And then she declared that she would not accompany me to church the next morning. Can you imagine her surprise when a boy so like our Ben in age and build, just fell upon us? Just moments after her declaration?"

I laughed, but when I saw his stern face, I stopped. We stared at each other for a long moment.

Then he drifted back behind his paper, saying, "We did not do for you son, you did for us. All that we have given you, we already had. But what you gave us that day—well, you gave us what we had lost, and thought never to see again."

What can you say to this? Except, "Yes, sir," and inwardly vow to be the best man you possibly can. I didn't know Ben but came to learn that he had a cheerful nature and every morning kissed Murlona on her cheek before going to school.

I accompanied my friends to the soda fountain after school and the pictures on Saturday nights. There were dances and parties and summers swimming in the quarry. And finally, there was high school graduation, yearbooks to sign, and bags to pack.

I told you, you may remember, I became a healer. Early and Murlona sent me to Iowa State University to study animal husbandry, and then on to veterinary school. Yes, this had been Ben's intended path. But I traveled it happily. How could I not? I was glad to step upon a road, knowing exactly where I would end up.

In the college town of Ames, way to the north of my adopted home, I saw my Millie for the first time. It was a Tuesday and I had stopped for lunch at a diner near the university. She wore a yellow dress the color of the lemon meringue pie I was gobbling. I watched her as she drank coffee and ate chicken salad on a wedge of iceberg lettuce. Turning the pages of a fashion magazine, she did not once look at me. But oh, how I watched her. The way her slim fingers hovered over a page. The way she tapped her white sandal to the beat of the jukebox. How her black hair trailed past her shoulders. When she finished, I followed her out and watched her climb behind the wheel of a Chrysler LeBaron, the same yellow as her dress. Never before had I looked at a girl and not known where her dress began and her car ended.

I looked for that yellow car on campus for weeks. It took me so long to find it because it was parked in the one place I didn't think to look: the University president's driveway. My Millie, you see, was the president's daughter. And yes, this darling, this golden girl became mine. Her father was none-too-pleased that she had thrown her lot in with an Iowa farm boy. But it was of no matter to us. Love has a way of protecting one from the outside, does it not? Sweet oblivion is what we had.

You must be wondering—how could you not—what my Millie said when I told her of the road. Of the jungles and the boxcars. The stealing and the picking. Vic the Viking and Teeny the porcelain girl. Yes, I know, you had to ask this question, but you may not like my answer.

I did not tell my Millie of that life. Instead, I told her of Uncle Early and Aunt Murlona, of how they would love her. I regaled her with stories of life on the farm, and how the rhythm of the animals changed against the backdrop of day, then night. She did not roll her eyes when I asked whether she wanted a brick or stucco mansion, and she laughed and called me silly when I told her on our first date that I would marry her.

Don't you see? I had to be the boy she thought she met. The man she loved. I was not—am not—ashamed of my life on the road. But if I told her, what was she to do with this knowledge? Tuck it into a winter coat with mothballs? Plant it in a garden? No. You cannot tell of such a thing and then expect that it will be anywhere except right in front of you, for all time. We all have our secrets. You have yours. You are thinking of them right now.

Teeny went into hibernation then, disappearing from my mind and into the basement of my brain. Don't you see? I could not be sad if I wanted to love my Millie. And I wanted to love someone. I wanted to love Millie.

You are wondering about the raffle baby because I have not mentioned the babe in some time. And so you tell yourself—of course you do—that Teeny was not gone from me for good.

Chapter Fifteen

B ut for now, I am still telling you of the courtship with my Millie, which unfolded during the war.

Your first question, the puzzle in your mind, might be why did I not go to serve in Europe or the Pacific? Why was I not sent to Africa? Why could I be safe in the arms of my Millie when my friends were sent away? You see, when doctors and nurses and veterinarians went off to war, someone had to stay on the home front to administer to the citizenry. It was that simple. By the time my veterinary course was set, the military was no longer enlisting veterinary students as officers to serve once their schooling was done. All around me, young veterinary students were dissuaded from enlisting. They had no opportunity to soldier for their country or show their courage. They could not leave behind the white feather of cowardice assigned to them. If you took their temperatures, the mercury would have registered black.

I did not join in the disappointment my fellow students shoul-dered when they could not go off to fight the Nazis. You see, I felt, and still do, that I had served my time already. Three years to be exact. How so, you wonder. I had not given limb (though others of my ilk had), but in three years of hoboing, I was not a burden on an already burdened government. The place I *did not* take in a soup line would have gone, perhaps, to a father with hungry children. The Salvation Army bed I did not sleep in was open for another boy of twelve, who did not have the benefit of friends and protection. I did not steal from the poor, thereby pushing them into government relief, such as that was. This may seem small to you but use your mathematics and add up three years of this and you will see that I made my sacrifice. I served my time. And what of that forced killing of innocents so many years ago in a field in Morris Township, Kansas? Surely, that in itself was service enough. I was a soldier drafted into an impossible war against Mother Nature.

But let us put aside those images and return to happier times.

Those days when I wooed my Millie, I diligently washed off the blood and the smell of formaldehyde fluid before I touched her elbow to steer her into the movie theater. I worked amid beakers, dog skeletons and horse autopsies, but I did not speak to her of bone or tissue. I wanted her only to see me clean and shiny. In hindsight, I see this choice was part of my quest to be the best man I could be. Like Early. Like Vic. I could not be courageous on the field of battle, but is it not so that sometimes, courage is simply doing what needs to be done?

The home front was marked by an interesting deprivation. I say interesting because while it was not unlike what I had experienced on the road, at least in concept and thought, it was different in design. Early and I planted and tended a victory garden over an acre large, and Murlona harvested, canned, and dried food until her fingers were stained by tomato juice and dried out by pickle brine.

War-time deprivation is methodical and organized. Yes. You know me too well. This is just how I liked it. I liked a line for sugar. The rigors of a ration book. It buoyed my soul that I could have precisely two-and-a-half pounds of meat per week. I liked rules. My heart sang a little louder with every mile I drove below the speed limit to save gas and rubber.

The summers of our courtship, while my Millie spent weeks at her family's summer lake home in Minnesota, I shadowed the doctor who tended to Early's livestock. He was so old that the army did not want him. His hands were similar to mine today in hue and translucence. And in steadiness, or lack thereof. Truth be told, he could no longer operate for the shaking, so under his tutelage, I performed the spays and neuters and tended to newborns and sewed up gashes. I administered to bloat, broken legs, scratched corneas, ear mites, and so on. All the while the old doctor observed and instructed, a hovering figure.

Early had taken on a part-time hired hand when I went away to college, but whenever I returned I fell back into the rhythm of the farm and helped where I was asked. Mostly, to tell the truth, I was inside with Murlona. One summer I painted her kitchen cabinets the same yellow as my Mille's dress that day at the diner. I helped my foster mother re-pot the violets that sat in her kitchen windowsill where they soaked in the morning sun, the blooms looking like candied flowers.

My Millie was a summer visitor from time to time, stealing away from Minnesota, shortening by a few days her father's attempt to keep us apart. She brought me white papery bark she had peeled from a birch tree. She would help Murlona put supper on the table and let Early beat her at checkers.

I knew she wore a navy bathing suit spotted with white daisies, for I had helped pick it out as we shopped one afternoon in Des Moines. I imagined her admiring herself in the mirror behind the fitting room curtain. It would be two years until graduation, when the curtain would be drawn back and she invited me in.

If you look too long at yourself in the mirror, eventually your eyes will see only what is behind you. I knew this, from those first days with Early and Murlona. And so, on my wedding day, I looked long enough only to shave and smooth my hair.

Ladies speak of weddings and babies. And even older ladies speak of viewings and funeral food. What can I say of my wedding day? I was twenty-five, and it was June 14, 1948. My Millie wore an ivory dress with a corsage of yellow roses at her wrist. When I rested my hand against her back, I felt the track of tiny pearl buttons along her spine. Her dark hair, once long to her shoulders, pixied around her ears. Early was my best man. And Murlona beamed knowingly. For so many years ago, in a downtown department store, she had outfitted me with the trappings of a future I could not yet see.

After our wedding, we moved to the small caretaker's cottage on the farm—a wedding gift from my foster parents—and settled into married life.

So, then. What of my life all the years when I was a newlywed, then faithful husband, then proud father to my sweet daughter? There is much to tell, but no reason to tell it all. I will give you meaning and depth rather than the play-by-play detail. I suppose you wonder how I can distill decades into a mere few hundred words. It is difficult, but I believe you could do it, too. You see, I built my life before the emergence of Facebook. No, you won't find me there, despite the effort of my granddaughter, my little Mia. I reflect on chunks of time, not moment by moment. It is enough that you will have my broad strokes, like stripes and medals on a military uniform. These tell you rank and tell you what and tell you where and perhaps with whom, and sometimes why, but not how. You don't need to know my how. It's not like that with me.

Broad strokes.

Here they are.

There were my twenties, when I feverishly built my animal practice, and almost every day with my Millie was a honeymoon. My thirties, where I joined the Rotary and led the Chamber of Commerce and welcomed my sweet Evelyn to the world. My forties, when I was wise and held in such high regard that vet students came to me in droves as interns. My fifties, when I watched my Millie tame her graying hair, and we took Spanish lessons at the community college. I retired in my sixties and we took a cruise to Alaska, and later accosted seven European countries in five days. I settled into pro bono work. My seventies. Well, stay with me. I will get to them later. My eighties were no different. My nineties. Well, you know of them. After all, I ramble on, and we are here together.

For now, hear this phrase: "Of an evening."

That was the substance of the life I made with my Millie.

Say it aloud. "Of an evening."

Do you feel the pull of softness and security of these words? The even keel of gentle and sweet? I took my Millie to the supper club, of an evening, and we danced so close there could be no breeze between us. I sat with my daughter and her multiplication tables, or caught fireflies, of an evening. I read veterinary journals by the fire, of an evening.

My life was like yours: a cycle. Some (perhaps you) yearn for surprise and adventure. But I relished the predictable rhythm of my life, and when I saw the symbols of days and seasons, contentment seared into me. We welcomed the new year at the country club. Stacks of pancakes declared it was Saturday. Pretty pedal pushers heralded the onset of summer. Little girl patent leather shoes and white cardigans meant Easter visiting time. The clink of ice in my Old-Fashioned glass told me to sink into my recliner, for it was Friday and I had earned it.

I see my Millie now. Brow furrowing as she contemplates a recipe in the *Ladies Home Journal*. I wish you could see her as I did. Her beehive practically crunched when she put her head on my pillow. I never saw so much hair spray in my life. She has moved to the record player to find Tony Bennett, Glen Campbell, or one of the many crooners who made her smile and sway, just as I always did.

And there was my sweet Evelyn, with her scraped knees and

lollipop lips, climbing into my lap for stories. I let her watch while a calf was born, and showed her how to follow the cattle market, just as Early had shown me. Later, there were slammed doors, rolling eyes, tearful good-byes, and happy reunions. My daughter called Early and Murlona Grandma and Grandpa, for what else would she call them? It wasn't until my own grandchildren were born that I understood what that meant to them.

I spent my career in atonement for the rabbits of so long ago. How could I not? You can imagine the quickening of my pulse when a little girl, a yellow ribbon in her hair and a tiny wrinkle on her forehead, brought her pet rabbit to me for inspection. In its red eyes, I saw reflected the rise of a club. Its ears twitched in rhythm to the thwack on a skull.

And so, I switched my focus to a large animal practice, heading out to farms and ranches at all hours. The squawk of chickens and the braying of a goat drowned memory. And this is how I doctored and calved year by year. I loaded my needle with nectar, and though I could control its trajectory, the liquid sometimes never reached its destination. But I did my best. Each patient, each creature, was one of those poor souls I had slaughtered. I could not bring them back. I could not change what I had done. But I could save their furry, braying brethren. And so I did.

I was not a hard man, but I did have one rule that could not be negotiated or broken. Food was not to be wasted. If you put it on your plate, you ate it. If you dropped a sandwich on the floor, you ate it. My only squabble with my Millie was over food, over the abundance of cake and ice cream made for birthday parties. Over the thirty hot dogs and thirty hamburger patties made for a July fourth neighborhood picnic. She was always afraid that we would not have enough to serve our guests. But mostly, she was afraid that it would reflect badly upon us as hosts if we ran out of food. This I understood. For I was tenderhearted, and she was so well intentioned that while I would not see past her excesses, I could let them co-exist with my commandment. In almost fifty years of marriage we learned to compromise. She made as much holiday and party food as she wanted, but we ate the leftovers at the family table until they were gone. One Christmas, my Millie made so many extra cookies and pies that even my sweet Evelyn and her friends tired of eating them, just as I had tired of strawberries, having eaten my fill as I harvested them so many years ago.

Was the memory of Teeny still difficult in those full, solid years of my life? Of course, but it came only sparingly. As you well know, there are rail tracks everywhere, yet sometimes I could pass them by and for long times resist thinking of those days. For my mind was occupied with the business of the present, which demanded my full attention: my child needed braces on her teeth. An entire herd of cattle needed my immediate attention. A coming snow threatened to land waist high in a February that followed a deadly January. I overextended myself with committees and clubs and organizations until I thought they might eat me alive. Is it the same for you? The present so greedy it elbows out all other thoughts. Think of your high school sweetheart. Of your college first love. Your brain could fathom nothing else at that moment.

During all those decades, I kept my counsel and still did not speak to anyone about riding the rails and hoboing with Teeny and Vic. Speaking a thing aloud creates a beginning and an end. When you speak a story in the air for another to hear, at some point, you stop. Keeping it locked in my heart, it was something just for me. And it would go on forever, no matter what. Teeny would always be with me, and that is what I wanted. I did not pine for her or cry for her. Nor did I cry for myself. It was not like that, see? You must not get the wrong idea. I loved Teeny. Of course. I still do. But I loved my Millie. I never yearned for Teeny, not in the way that deposits stones in your gut. As the years went by her absence no longer created a void. But the place she occupied would never find another occupant. I was not foolish enough to think I would see her again. And as those beautiful early married years went by, Teeny did not inhabit my mind but rather visited it from time to time, coming back to me in little places. In the bottle of nail polish and make-up compact resting on my Millie's dressing table. In the wail of a train whistle, so imperceptible but still a bee in my ear. It would take me many years to realize that she remained with me because I had never had the chance to say good-bye. If I had one regret during those years, it was that we had not told each other "farewell."

And what of Vic? You haven't forgotten him, have you? Perhaps you think *I* have. No, for I could not think of Teeny without thinking of him. I never did see him again. I never knew his real name, or where he lived with his foster family. And I never knew if he made it to the CCC in Utah or not.

And Roley. Did I ever think of Roley? Was I plagued with guilt? You already know the answer to that question. But from time to time he came to me like a clenched fist in my gut when I remembered his head under water, his legs flaying about for purchase. I don't believe I told you what happened after we left him. We simply walked away. Note my word choice. We walked. We did not run. Sometimes in the early days with the Zugs, as I lay awake at night, I heard the steady crunch of my feet over dead leaves as I followed Vic back to the migrant camp from the stream where we left Roley. We stole back to our bedroll nests and burrowed in. I saw an eye open and close. I heard a boy turn in his sleep.

Chapter Sixteen

Are you wondering why I call the ladies of my life "my Millie" and "my sweet Evelyn"? I know, I know. In this day and age that is not done. But do not mistake my affection for dominance. I did not possess them, they possessed me. I needed them far more than they ever needed me, though I don't believe they knew this.

My granddaughter, my little Mia, is forty now and strong and proud like her mother and grandmother.

When she was little she asked me for my family tree for a school project. I gave her branches, twigs and roots that sprung from magic beans, and sharpened my made-up stories to the point of a long-ago childhood crayon. And it took me years to fully realize that my fictional past was a kaleidoscope of fairytales, like Teeny's, created for the benefit of others.

I maintained the tale Early and Murlona had concocted: that I was their nephew, taken in when my parents died in a car crash in Virginia.

I told my little Mia of the smart new shoes my mother never gave me each new school year; how the leather shone like a lucky copper penny. I exaggerated the satisfactory tug of new laces. I conjured Labor Day potato salad spiked with fresh dill, and pungent fig cakes that never held even one birthday candle. I spoke of traditions we never followed: sauerkraut, pork, and black-eyed peas to bring luck in the New Year. And delivering hampers to the poor on Christmas Eve.

And do you know what the child did? These are her gifts to me: I ride along in the car when she delivers baskets of food to our down-and-out church parishioners, even though I am slow and my cane taps out a sloth's journey to and from the car. Every New Year's Eve she sets my table with a white cloth and Murlona's good china, and we slip a pork roast into my oven. She lets me stir the sauerkraut and soak the beans while she makes an apple strudel. On my birthday, she bakes a spicy fig cake in one of Murlona's old Bundt pans. She delivers it, still warm, with a cup of rum icing we pour on top, immediately before devouring two slices each. I had no family recipes to hand down to her. But I suppose that is what the internet is for.

These are my treats now: she is a one-of-a-kind child. You have one too, who surprises and delights you until your heart beats, not with blood, but a golden, liquid joy. Oh, how she reminds me of Murlona with her sensible, loving ways and her modest self-deprecation.

Murlona. When is the last time I spoke to you of Murlona, my generous and loving foster mother? Her spirit surrounds me still, as befits a matriarch who bequeathed me all she had, after devoting her life to my happiness. She is in the cut glass butter dish and matching salt and pepper shakers, which I remember her ordering from the Sears catalog, and which grace my kitchen table. Do you recall the violets she kept on the windowsill of her kitchen, the ones that bewitched me with their candy-like blooms? Oh, they have long since died, but I rooted cuttings year after year and there are three or four generations of Murlona's violets in my kitchen.

How to love unconditionally—this was Murlona's most enduring gift to me. It was Murlona who showed me how to cherish and care for my Millie, for I simply mimicked how she cared for Early.

Murlona stripped the corn kernels off the cob and into a golden pile on Early's dinner plate, for he preferred it that way. She did not fuss when he forgot to take off his boots before crossing her just-washed kitchen floor. Come tax season, he might come home from work and head straight to the liquor cabinet and pour a whiskey. Those evenings, Murlona called me down from my room and told me to finish the remaining farm chores. Then she would bring Early's dinner to him on a tray, as he sat in his favorite chair, feet upon a hassock. Each summer she visited her sister on the central California coast, and always returned with a box of his favorite salted taffy. Although love lived mostly in unspoken gestures as far as Murlona was concerned, she did have a favorite phrase reserved just for Early. She would say "you're probably right," even when we all—including Early—knew he wasn't. Murlona explained the power of these words to me once I was married. That phrase could end an argument, ease a guilty conscious, and reverse a turned back, she said. And it could prevent a word that once spoken cannot be unsaid.

When my Millie was with child, I thought often of my orphaned friends. It had not occurred to me before then, but neither Teeny, Vic, nor I had spoken to each other of our parents. This was partly, I was certain, because it was writ large in the hobo code that you did not ask where a 'bo was from, only where he was headed. Of course, Teeny and Vic had parents. I imagined they were of no consequence, like mine.

As my Millie tossed and turned in bed in her ninth month, I tried to make her comfortable, rearranging her pillows under her back and feet, until finally I relinquished my own and she could sleep. As my Millie slept, I thought of all my restless nights with

Teeny and Vic on bedrolls and newspapers, shivering to stay warm. When we had the resources, we had always taken special care of Teeny. We would pitch a tarpaulin tent for her, tree branches for the polls and an extra blanket to warm her. For, after all, she was a girl.

It was my Millie, really, who made sure I didn't become like my own father. No, she did not know the truth, but I think she sensed my hesitation, for she was quick to reassure me. She believed that I would be a good father, and so I was. I came to learn, early on, that if my Millie believed something, well, it was so. I would jokingly ask her to believe that we would win a car or enough money for our toddler's college education. But she would just smile her wickedly mysterious smile—the one I know she smiled that day behind the dressing room curtain—and tell me that it did not work that way.

Two pieces of my past remained with me: Vic's worn *Reader's Digest* and the one-dollar bill he left the day we parted. I kept the *Reader's Digest* in my safe. The dollar bill was tucked in my wallet behind my driver's license. But it is not there still.

One Sunday morning, my Millie needed money for the collection. I was out on a call but had left my wallet behind. Yes, what you suspect happened did happen. My lucky one-dollar bill, one half of my physical connection to Vic and Teeny, ended up in the plate at the First United Methodist Church. It was a few years until I knew it was missing. One year, my sweet Evelyn gave me a handsome new wallet for Father's Day, and I dutifully transferred contents from the old, under the pleased and proud watchfulness of my daughter. When I saw that the dollar bill was missing, I felt a marble fall into my stomach and roll around. I felt it roil, slow, and then stop. Later, I asked my Millie about it, and she confessed. She was desperately unhappy when she saw my angst. But of course, I could not tell her the truth, so I told her it was my lucky bill, a gift from Early, and left it at that.

The circle of life came back around for Early when my sweet Evelyn was just nine and did not understand that she would never see her grandfather again.

When I gazed upon Early's face in his casket, I was relieved that what I saw was what I had seen that first winter together. I was transported back to those frigid, blustery days, when his nose was the red of wind burn. While he went about his farm chores, he wore a black and orange checked hat, its sheepskin earflaps and peak brought down and buttoned around his face to spite the elements. That hat still hung on a peg in Murlona's kitchen. And I knew it would stay there, where she could look at it every day and smile or cry.

I shifted my feet as I peered into the casket. I looked down to Early's hands, rough with his farm work, folded together over his chest like an X. I stared at them until my vision blurred. Then I saw them moving the tassel on my mortar board the day I graduated from high school. Slipping me folded bills whenever I came home from college. Holding his granddaughter at the baptismal font. And then I reached out and touched his arm. It was my salute. I did not see death that day because I did not want to. I brought memory with me to Early's funeral. And then I brought it home to give Murlona.

Murlona insisted on moving into the caretaker cottage not long after we buried Early in the family plot. We protested, naturally, but she started packing her belongings, nonetheless. We knew she was serious when she began to carry the boxes across the driveway, her apron strings sailing behind her as if they were waving goodbye.

Our trio moved into the big house then. And as time wore on, my Millie would buff and polish the furniture and freshen Murlona's curtains until they were stiff with the starch she used on my Sunday shirts.

Returning to the big house was a step back in time for me. Yes, I had walked over there practically every day since my Millie and I married and moved into the cottage. But on that moving day after Early's death, with a box of pots and pans on my hip, I stopped to feel for the curled edge of the Formica table in Murlona's kitchen, just to make sure it was still there. I don't know what I would have done if it wasn't.

Chapter Seventeen

I t was very fashionable in the seventies and eighties for a man to have a mid-life crisis. My Millie used to tease me that I was born middle-aged, and I let her have this innocent fun at my expense. But no, I wasn't born a middle-aged man, I just got there three decades before I should have and settled there. So, my crisis of identity was not of who I was in my middle age. My identity crisis was always with me.

All those years in Murlona and Early's house and the cottage, I saw my face in the mirror every morning as I shaved. But of course, I never let my gaze linger very long for I did not want to see the lies and sins upon my face. I never did feel guilty for the food and clothes I stole. For the scams we pulled. Stealing and scamming, well, they were a first aid kit, and it was desperately needed. And we only did it when we were desperate. But I couldn't help but wonder what others saw when they looked at me. And they did look at me. It couldn't be helped, and I am not being vain, but like I already told you, I topped out at six foot four and everyone always looks at a giant, do they not? It can't be helped.

I told you, earlier, how busy I was in my forties. I think these were my sweetest years, when I had settled into life and possessed the necessary combination of wisdom, vibrancy, and fortitude. As a loving husband and doting father, I realized my love for Teeny had shifted. Years had worked away at puppy love, rearranging its very DNA and morphing it into something akin to the paternal love she had needed from me all along. It was thirty years too late, and Teeny was not there to receive it, but it brought me peace to know that I possessed it. And as long as it existed, there was the chance that I could give it to her after all. No matter its form, I still felt a deep kind of love that will always ask a question, until an answer is produced.

When my sweet Evelyn turned fifteen, the declared age of Teeny that first time I saw her in the hobo jungle, I began to study Evelyn closely, but oh, I was always too late. My daughter seemed to grow from babe to toddler to teen in the time it takes to butter toast.

Should we address the elephant in the room?

You want to know why I never looked for Teeny.

Where should I have looked? I did not know where we had been separated. I had no landmark other than a light blue water tower. I did not know her name or even where she came from. Geography had betrayed me.

I suppose since I could not look for Teeny, I looked for clues of her life in my own daughter.

When my sweet Evelyn pouted for some reason or another, I saw the petulant Teeny who was determined to rankle Vic. The day Richard Heller broke my daughter's heart in seventh grade, and she cried into my shoulder, I felt Teeny's head on my chest, where she sobbed as I told her about Roley and the dog. I felt her shoulder blade shift under my fingers.

As the years went on, with my sweet Evelyn busy with school and cheerleading, dances and concerts, my Millie discovered that she was interested in pottery and macramé. More and more my dinner was waiting in the warmer when I came home from work. It was in those silent moments, sitting at Murlona's Formica table,

I began to think more of Teeny. She would have been in her late forties. I imagined her fiery red hair pulled back into matronlyness. But no, that was not right. Teeny would not have been tamed. I could not imagine her any older than the day we lost each other. She would always be a slip of a teenage girl, dancing in orange shoes and silver bracelets.

My Millie used a special cream at night, applied with her fingertips against her temples. She said it cured the march of time. As I watched her in the vanity mirror, I thought of that expression. The march of time. I did not want to see wrinkles, grey hairs, or gnarled knuckles on Teeny, for they were an unpleasant blemish across my memory. I bade them stay away. But on my Millie, well, they just made her more beautiful to me.

The march of time did not stop even for my formidable foster mother. I was fortunate enough to have had Murlona in my life for three decades before she left us. After the arrangements and people and such, I went through Murlona's things and found a photo album she had tucked away in her nightstand drawer, pictures of me and Ben, with *My Sons* written on the cover. There are times when we are transported back to places in our past that can surface in an instant. I sat on Murlona's bed and wept, for I was the fifteen-year-old man-child again.

I buried Murlona in the family plot where she rested between Early and Ben, her reward for a life well-lived. After the mourners and preacher left the graveside, I arranged the flowers as I knew she would like them. Just so. I remembered the silly promise to care for her violets. I promised she would not be forgotten. And see. She is not. For you have given her your attention. And you will not forget. This is a story not easily dispatched to the outer limits of your mind.

When my sweet Evelyn was ready for college, my Millie and I drove to the city of Boone, in western North Carolina. Appalachian State University was, so I was told, one of the finest schools for the performing arts.

You have heard of Brigadoon, surely? That mystical town that is invisible all but once every hundred years, when it rises from the mist? And so it was when my sweet Evelyn, my Millie and I chugged up the mountains in western Carolina, singing rounds of *She'll Be Coming 'Round the Mountain When She Comes*. Me with my baritone, my Millie with her alto, my sweet Evelyn with her soprano. You remember this song, do you not? "Round the mountain. When she comes. She'll be driving six white horses when she comes. When she comes. She'll be wearing silk pajamas when she comes. When she comes."

On the chorus, the highway seemed to straighten and we drove past a small country store on the left. A quaint picture of men sitting on benches playing checkers. A woman wiped a baby's face as it grabbed for her ice cream cone. A dog roamed to and fro, looking for scraps. Road signs started to appear. And out of the mist—for it was a foggy morning—a sign for Elk Grove. It jogged my memory, but not to the point of total consciousness, for I was in North Carolina, after all, not Tennessee, where the gypsy prince had waited for Teeny. And then another tourist sign, with a large arrow for Grandfather Mountain appeared. Memory was not jogged now but jolted, and I felt that each of my organs was in a different room.

Can you just imagine the steady stream of circumstances, coincidences, decisions, and blind passions that came together and made the dominos of my life fall, just so? It started when I collapsed in Early and Murlona's kitchen. Without them there would have been no college, and without college I would not have met my Millie. Without her, there would be no sweet Evelyn, and without my daughter, I would never have stood under Grandfather Mountain on soil I knew had once supported Teeny. Without *Wonder Woman* and *Charlie's Angels* (television programs you may be too young to remember), my sweet Evelyn might have become an accountant or dental hygienist, instead of an actress.

I don't know what I expected to find. I didn't believe I would find her, my friend from yesteryear.

That afternoon, after we said good-bye to our daughter, I left my Millie at the hotel spa where she would be spit and polished with seaweed and rocks and whatever else could be dug up from water and earth. I lied to my wife that day. Besides the very falsehood of my life, I had never before lied to her. That day, I invented a story about a nearby large animal veterinarian and a new vaccination technique. God love her, my Millie was a good woman, a smart and quick soul, but by choice she was no scientist. Her eyes glazed over as soon as I said the word "injection," and so we parted, her to her seaweed, me in pursuit of a fairytale.

I walked throughout the town of Elk Grove, with its tree-lined streets and low stone walls. Middle-aged couples—I suspected new college parents like myself—wandered the main street, looking into shop windows, or enjoyed breakfast in the only diner in town.

Whenever I glanced up, I saw the Grandfather Mountain range that encircled the town, each dip and crevice forming a face here and there. The one distinct profile of the old man, the outcropping of rock where Teeny said she was to wait for her gypsy prince, went in and out of my line of sight.

I walked on aimlessly, past the one gas station, up a narrow alley, then back again, a circuitous route that brought me face-to-face with a small log cabin library, very much like the library in one of Teeny's stories. The logs were worn, but sturdy, and the bright white mortar most certainly had been recently applied.

In the three seconds it took me to place my fingers around the door handle, time stopped, and I bent it to my will so I could recall the memory and savor the words Teeny had shared in a jungle so many years before about a long-lost library that took prisoners.

Chapter Eighteen

"In the Great Smoky Mountains beyond a small Tennessee town, where streets were no wider than needles and people did not have names, there was a tiny log cabin library. Now this town had long been forgotten by the government, for it did not appear on any map. No one came knocking on doors to collect taxes, sell insurance or round up young men to join the army. The town was so high up and covered so completely by a canopy of thick trees, that no roads ran to or from it. The people had never seen a horse, ridden in a car, or felt the luscious sheen of silk.

"The land that surrounded the people provided a life that was both sweet and savory, and so happiness followed. The people of the tiny community hunted deer, wild boars, and small game. They collected hazelnuts, chestnuts, and walnuts. There were fish in the streams, berries on the bushes, and small sour apples that could be dried and eaten in the winter, along with rich salted pork. The maple trees gave of their syrup. The hardwoods allowed themselves to be cut and felled to make snug cabins, or to be burned to provide warmth. And the land provided magnolias and wild orchids, beauty to complete the people's lives. The lush moss all around them was like velvet, and the people put it on their roofs where it sang its song of green perfection.

"There was no predator on the heels of the town. No one coveted them and so no harm came to them from the outside. But still, the people spoke only in whispers, lest a man or woman down the mountain might hear them. And although this was highly unlikely, it was a precaution that seemed to be passed along to every new child. Children learned to speak in signs at first. Only when they were old enough to understand the ways of their clan did they learn to speak.

"But what of the library? How did there come to be a library in a place with no name, known to only a few dozen people who had never tasted chocolate, posed for a photograph, or heard a jazz band?

"Why, it had been there all along, that's how. Just long forgotten.

"When the little girl in this story discovered the library cabin, she had just woven strings of daisy chains into her golden hair and wandered far higher and deeper into the forest than she was allowed, for she had seen a bright red bird and wanted it to perch on her shoulder.

"The little girl was almost fourteen, though she did not know it. She knew only that she was of the age when it was time to watch her little sisters, grind corn into meal, and find a boy to live with.

"As she wandered high into the mountains, she lost her way. She knew the land would keep her safe, warm, and fed, but she was so tired when she stumbled onto the little cabin that she took its uncertain shelter. It looked not so different from the one she and her family occupied. Knowing it would not be light for much longer, she cleaned away the cobwebs and vines that covered the door and stepped inside. There was a little table and chair in the middle of the room, with a dusty fireplace and cot at the far end. The walls were covered, floor to ceiling, with shelves stuffed with books of all sizes and colors.

"Now the girl had only seen one book in her life. It was a sacred vessel that ate the peoples' sins, cured their sores and coughs, and cut off hands or blinded them when they had stolen from each other. Each family took turns keeping the book and passing on its lessons to the children, until the book, with its onion thin pages, was so delicate it could not be used anymore, and it was put away. This had happened several years previously, and the girl's family was the last to keep it.

"The people were better off without it, though, the girl thought, as she surveyed the rows of books in front of her. For since it had gone away, the book had not cut off a hand. None of her friends had been stoned.

"Naturally, the girl was afraid of all these books, and wanted nothing more than to leave. As soon as it was light the next day, she tried to find her way home. But her foray brought her back to the little cabin. Day after day, she left the cabin at first light, only to find herself back at dusk, exhausted from her wanderings. And always, those silent, unknowable sentinels waited on the shelves when she returned.

"Soon, the leaves turned into her favorite colors and she could hear the plop plop plop of acorns, so she began to do the things her mother had taught her to prepare for the winter. She used sharp rocks to fashion a spear, knives, fire starters and mortar and pestle. She completed each ritual of hunting, gathering, preparing, storing and planning, one by one, as if she had a list in front of her.

"The year ended. Another started. And then again. And again. It took the girl many years to read all the books, for it took her many years before she started reading. First, she thought perhaps it might be all right to just touch them. So far, they had not hurt her. But, before she opened any of them, she re-organized them by size. She took them all off the shelves and made piles on the floor. Then she broke off fir tree branches and swept the dust from the books and shelves. She re-ordered the books, from smallest to largest.

"The next winter, she re-arranged the books by color, still

unready to open them. Then she read the words on each of the book covers. Finally, after ten years, she opened one, and began to read. She started with the red books, for this, the color of berries, was her favorite. She moved on to green, brown, blue, yellow, white, and so on and so on. Each color reminded her of home. The green of the moss, the brown of her mother's hair, the yellow of the flowers that blanketed the sloping hills in the valley below her little town.

"Some of the books had pretty pictures of smiling people who, although their dress and manner were unfamiliar, looked kind. She tore these pages carefully from the books and kept them in a pile on the little table, a paper family that could be brought out for company. When she did not like a book, she put it aside to be dealt with later, and soon that pile grew, too.

"By the time she had read all of the books, another five years had passed. It took that long because she could not read all the time, as much as she wanted to. To survive, she had to complete her chores. She had to carry water many times over in a small bag she had made from deer hide. She had to dry meat and forage for mushrooms and tubers. She had to skin hides for clothes and shoes and make needles and cutlery from deer antlers. She was young enough that she felt like an adventurer she had read about in one of the books, and so she sometimes still tried to find her way home, only to find herself back at the little cabin no matter which way she went.

"The girl grew into middle age, and she no longer felt the need to wander. She felt the contentment that comes with acceptance. She turned to the pile of discarded books and tore out all the pages. The she began to fold them into shapes. At first, a squirrel looked like a flower and a house looked like a deer, but soon her fingers knew the way. She had become a creator, putting into her world the things that she wanted. She folded silver pages into a pretty skirt with a pocket, just like her mother had worn. She folded pages with numbers into a smokehouse. And with this newly discovered pastime, she was no longer just a girl who had survived and given in to a life not of her choosing. She was a maker of beauty, and she was proud of herself.

"When she had finished folding the last page from the last discarded book, she had built a paper town, like the one she had lost. Using tiny bone shards, she pinned each folded page to the log ceiling. When she lay on her bed staring up at what she had done, she thought about the people she used to know, and wondered if they had ever looked for her.

"Then she read all of the books again, from the very beginning, starting with the first red book. But this time, she read the books aloud to her paper friends. At first her voice sounded like a scratch, but soon it returned to its beautiful self, and she relished the strength she had not known it had. She learned that she could change her voice to match the personality of a person in a book. And she was happy, because she no longer felt so alone.

"It wasn't until the third time she read the books that she understood them and knew that each occupied its own particular place in the larger world.

"For years, she had matched words from one book with pictures from another. And this is how she learned what a light bulb was, and that it was the lightning outside that made it shine. She learned how to make pretty dresses and hats, but of course did not have the materials to do so. She learned that there were such things as cities, and if she stood on a street and put out her arm, a car would stop and take her anywhere she wanted to go. And oh, how she wanted to go. It took some time, but she learned the shape of the continents, and from a book with a language she did not understand printed alongside words she knew, she learned where she lived on the maps, and how far she would have to travel to ride a camel, dance around a maypole and cross a desert of wind-swept sand.

"The more she understood, the sadder she became. She was surrounded by the life she wanted and the things she craved, but she could not have them. She could not crawl into the pages to eat sweets, dance with handsome men, or watch a dolphin slip in and out of ocean waves. She stopped reading when she discovered that using bird feathers, juice from berries, and the blank pages in the books, she could write the letters she saw, and someone else could read and understand them. It almost broke her heart to know that even if she wrote her story, no one would ever see it. But maybe she would try it anyway.

"When the girl died, she was an old woman with no teeth. She had not read a book for so many years that she might as well have forgotten how. When men eventually came up the mountain to take the hardwood that grew for miles and miles around her cabin, they found her bones on a rotted mattress made of deer hide and grasses. When they started going through her things, they found that she had written a story on blank pages torn from the books that were rotting on the shelves encircling the room. The men were careless, and only wanted the hardwood, not the dusty, decrepit artifacts of an old woman, long dead. But one of them thought it might be worth a few dollars that he could drop at the dog track, so he wrapped the pages in a wrinkled deer hide.

"When he showed the pages to his wife that evening, she said they were of no value. And because she had gone to secretarial school, he believed her. After supper, his wife made sure he watched as she placed the bundle in the rubbish bin in the kitchen. Once he had left for work the next morning, she took the bundle and wrapped it in butcher's paper, securing it with string, and slipped the package through the mail slot at the county historical society on Hickory Street."

Chapter Nineteen

W hen my memory completed Teeny's story, time was bent back to its proper place, and I turned the knob and walked into the Elk Grove library. Of course, the little town library was not anything like the library in Teeny's fairytale.

I will tell you a secret, but you must promise not to laugh. When I stepped inside and saw computer stations, a rack of DVDs, and a photocopy machine, there surfaced a disappointment I had not felt in my heart since the day Roley first doffed his cap to Teeny. It's funny, isn't it, that you can be disappointed despite not harboring any expectations?

I browsed the shelves, lingering in the local history section, and pulled volumes arbitrarily. A friendly librarian settled me at a corner table. Seeing my stack of local history tomes, she pushed an over-sized folio to me and left me to my task. I opened it to an arbitrary page and leafed through a collection of photographs, letters, newspaper articles and such, celebrating the one hundredth anniversary of the town of Elk Grove.

Can you guess what happened next? What could be so important that I found it sitting at a tiny far-away library?

133

Well, dear friend. I found the raffle baby.

You did not expect this, did you? You did not expect this sentence.

I will say it again.

I found the raffle baby.

Yes, you are correct. The very one that Teeny told us about in that California migrant camp. The story no one believed.

As I scanned headlines I came across the following: "Methodist Church Raffle."

The article declared: *"Purchase your ticket for a chance to win a rosy-cheeked little one. Ladies particularly welcome."*

What do you do when proof of a past far gone drops in your lap? So far gone that perhaps it doesn't even matter? So, Teeny was the raffle baby all along. Of all her stories, how wild and wonderful that this was the one that was true! I scanned the rest of the article and saw that it was published in 1934. But I had met Teeny in 1936. And just like that, an answer found was an answer lost.

I looked around the library and out the small window from which one could see Grandfather Mountain looming heavenward. Surely Teeny had been here at some point. While all of her stories were set in the Smoky Mountains of Tennessee, I knew for certain that here in North Carolina I walked in her footsteps.

I couldn't think of what to do next, so I showed the young librarian the article and she laughed and shrugged. She had just moved to the area last year, she said. The former librarian, who had been in her post for sixty years, had recently died. My mind flashed back to old Opal Mae in the Sioux City library. My nightmare and Teeny's fairytale had collided.

I asked the girl to photocopy the page, and carefully placed a dime on the reference desk.

For the rest of the afternoon, I strolled around the town. There was an old-fashioned drug store still open, with a pharmacist who appeared to be as old as Moses. I wandered in and asked him about the article. I took it from my pocket, unfolded it and put it in front of him.

"Memory's not what it used to be, son," he said, counting pills. "You might ask at the library."

I inquired about the cloistered St. Mary's convent and the gypsy caravan. I asked about all the names and landmarks I could remember from Teeny's stories, but the old man had not heard of even one. I asked about a rolling hill covered with yellow flowers and an old donkey trail favored by the gypsies. The old man just shook his head and sighed. For I had made him lose his counting place, and he had to start over.

At the newspaper office, the editor ushered me in and moved piles of papers so that I could sit and show him the article. Like the librarian, he was a young man. He could do no more than pull out a copy of the original paper on microfilm, allowing me to touch a fantasy with only my eyes. I was chasing ghosts and fairies, I decided. What use was it trying to ask people to remember things I knew they had never even seen and would never even know? These were the shards of truth and lies I bid you to find when I first started this tale. I felt I was back at that unknown place where I had first lost Teeny, under a bright moonlight, which shone upon angry bulls and a light blue water tower.

Chapter Twenty

I returned home with my Millie the next day, for there had been no parting in the fog and therefore Brigadoon had not revealed itself. No trace of a gypsy girl or orphaned child wearing a sash the color of a buttercup. No magical library that took prisoners and held them for a lifetime. Surprisingly, this did not weigh heavy on me. For in a way I had found at least a trace of Teeny. The article might have been true, but I was certain Teeny had embellished it beyond recognition. Teeny had always been the child of mystery and the bride of lies. Why would that have changed with the passage of time?

I put the photocopy of the newspaper article in my office safe, next to insurance papers, passport and similar documents that tell me who I am and what I want. I had to keep it, you see, somewhere close where I could consult it, but not so close that it could watch me and tell me that time was passing by.

For I already knew that. And how fast twenty-five years are whittled away, like a laser burns through driftwood.

I thought I was old then, when I was seventy-two, never knowing that I would live decades longer and be sitting here with you, telling my tale, rehashing old times.

When my sweet Evelyn graduated from college, she married, had children, and settled into teaching drama in Chicago. Soon her family moved west and returned only on holidays. It is distance that kills love and intimacy. You know this story. It plays out a thousand times. But then my little Mia, my dear granddaughter, came to visit on her own. First for summers. Then for college. Then to stay.

As the years passed in my happy marriage, the frantic love of youth settled into mature love. Mature love is the carousel horse with the chipped ear and the faded paint. Despite the wear and tear, its course remains steady. And its eyes do not close, though the merry-go-round music might be harder to hear. In mature love, there is a lot of room for other pursuits. There is more time on the golf course. You can finally sleep when your wife is reading in bed with the lamp on. And of course, the noise of everyday life slows. The rush in the ears lessens. There is again room for memory and reflection.

That final decade I spent with my Millie was filled with that mature love. But like my love for Teeny, it snaked around us, shedding a skin or two. Some days, the love of the early days still came to breakfast. But companionship was what we savored in those years, and what we whispered about before falling asleep: the trail we would walk the next day, the bridge game we had lost that afternoon, the gift certificate we needed to use. We reminded each other of doctor's appointments. My Millie watched my sodium. I steadied her as she climbed the stairs. We laughed when we could not remember what we had eaten for dinner the evening before.

Cancer took my Millie in 1998, just days before our fiftieth wedding anniversary party. She asked me to have the party without her and teased me that all the food we had ordered would go to waste if I did not. Instead, my little Mia arranged for it to go to needy families.

My little Mia coaxed me through the pain. It's ironic, we all eventually must speak the language of grief, but no one knows what to say. There is a finite supply of words that we can take to the graveside or sickroom. Sometimes, my little Mia just sat with me in a quiet contemplation. She never offered something she did not have.

Then there came the day, as I went about my morning chores alone and missing my Millie, that I told her all about my hobo days. The salt and pepper shakers and cereal boxes, they listened too. Yes, that was a joke. Did you find it funny? I felt her all around me, but yes, I knew she was no longer with me in the physical realm.

I told my Millie about my start in life and how I slept on wrestling mats before riding the rails. I watered Murlona's violets and told her about finding Vic, and Teeny finding us. About the fairytales and villains on the road. I broke down when I told her about the dog that Roley killed, and the rabbits I had murdered. I begged for her forgiveness because I knew she would give it.

She would have asked about the things I carried with me, so I dug up the old *Reader's Digest* Vic had left me and showed her the train schedules and the signs. She would have been marked as a kind lady in residence. We would have had a steady stream of 'boes in our house for a sit-down meal from dawn to dusk. And my Millie would have treated them all like they were Frank Sinatra come to call.

After my supper of leftover pot roast, I treated myself to a dish of vanilla ice cream. I used Murlona's favorite spoon, the sole survivor of a set of eight. Silver in infancy, it had aged to a dull grey, but it still tapered to a narrow tip, and Murlona had favored it when she made trifles or puddings. They were her crowns, the spoon a scepter.

Then I brought out the newspaper article, soiled with oil from my restless fingers, about the raffle baby, and I told my Millie that story. And then, I couldn't stop. I told her about the little girl nun and the gypsy child. I told her about the library and the little girl who froze to a tree and the orphan who died from happiness the very day she was adopted.

I saved the worst for last. I told her about the too-big boots and the bull who snatched Teeny by the waist and hauled her away over his shoulder like she was a sack of potatoes.

It felt good to tell the story. Yes, I spoke it aloud. But no one heard. And so, it was still only mine.

But now. Now you are hearing the story. It has started its slow descent.

Chapter Twenty-One

You are still here! Do you wonder at my surprise? You see, I know how busy you are. There. I see the list in your mind: three loads of laundry, a broken dishwasher, an unfinished Halloween costume, twenty cupcakes to bake, and homemade icing to whip up because you are a perfectionist and store-bought will not do. There is the lawn to tame and the fall leaves to persuade into the oversize leaf bags. Yes. You are a trooper to have remained this long.

After my Millie went and my knees began protesting the stairs in the big house, I took my boxes to the cottage, and it was my little Mia who freshened my curtains and ironed them into starched panels. She settled into the big house with her husband and children.

There. I can see my little Mia and her children in the garden. Sometimes they wave. Yes, I do love them, but imagine what children can do to an old man's bones.

My little Mia and her husband commute into the city for busy jobs, but she finds time for me in-between the children's soccer games and birthday parties. She looks at me, but she does not see the man I am. But how could she? I never told her that my character was forged on the anvil of steel rails and stolen pies. But no mind. My little Mia sees her Poppy and I am the recipient of her goodness.

One day I might put this tale to paper, now that I have poured it out into the world for you. And so my Mia can really know me. But for now, I am happy that you are my first listener. It has been a pleasure to travel this far with you.

But I am ahead of myself. For I haven't yet told how I came to bring our story full circle. How I found Teeny after so many years.

After my Millie's death, new tendrils of memory surfaced, as if released on the seeds of her passing. Do you know it took me sixty years to remember, or recall (for they are different beasts), that I had told Teeny where I was from? All those years ago I had shouted my name as the bull drug her kicking and screaming. I yelled so loud that I could see my lungs in the puffs of breath, so surely she must have heard me. And I had told her the name of my hometown.

"You are an old fool," I told myself, as I boarded a plane to Pittsburgh.

"What do you expect to find?" I asked myself as I completed the rental car application and drove down Route 66 toward my hometown. How different the city was, my first city where I had met Vic. I hardly recognized it.

I knew as soon as I crossed the county line into Connellsville that Teeny was not there—that she had not even been there. The air would have been different. The main street, where I had soiled comic books so many decades earlier, surely would have been paved with gold had she walked across the cobblestone street and slate sidewalks.

But still, I had come all this way. So I did not look for her. Instead, I looked for myself. The elementary school where I had slept before I hit the rails was a crumbled building of chipped brick and smashed windows. When did it get so small? It had been vast with echoes and ghosts when I wandered the halls, looking for cafeteria scraps and despairing over the broken water fountains.

Hoffman's Drugstore was gone, pushed out no doubt by the chain store around the corner. In its place stood a trendy fashion shop with a coffee bar in the back. I ordered a cappuccino just so I could say I had done so once in my life. I laughed at the smiley face the girl swirled in the foam. How many trifles like these had I missed? Please, hear me. I hope you do not miss these in your life. Love the simplicity that is gentle around you. A pretty cup of coffee. A sprig of bittersweet upon a mantle. A scraggly weed that bears a purple flower. A prime parking space in a pouring rain.

I went to the only cemetery in town and found my mother's grave. I knew if she was anywhere, she would be there. There was no resting place beside her for my father, so I was made to think he never returned to her.

Her tombstone was simple grey granite. It read: "Beatrice C. Giles, 1876-1941. Forgive Me."

I remained there a long while, standing on decades as if they were mere seconds. The harsh topography of my mother's face flashed in front of me. I remembered limp bologna sandwiches on bread sliced so thin, it was practically translucent. I saw the hollow ache in eyes that stopped seeing me. How was it possible that I did not possess even one happy memory of the years I lived with my parents? Even the long-ago yo-yo, made by my father for my sixth birthday, was a scarred memory because he had stolen the wood to make the wheel.

In the distance, I heard the train whistle blow. In my mind, I followed the sound down past the mill to the place I had jumped my first boxcar. Had this train not been going so fast, I might have grabbed the catwalk, just as I had done years before. I had been a boy of twelve that first time, holding on as if I was hanging on to the needle of a compass.

I recognized so little of my hometown. But most importantly, it did not fit in that place inside me where home is birthed and carried. No, that was back in Iowa. When I returned home, I promised myself, I would go to the family plot just beyond the barn. My little Mia would help me weed around the headstones. I would see Murlona and Early and my Millie. We would be together, at home.

I did not fly back to Iowa. You see, when you are not in a hurry, you hear and feel things that otherwise would pass you over. I would be home soon enough, and something about that train whistle made me want to slow down.

You will see. You will be glad I did.

Chapter Twenty-Two

I drove home on the back roads and by-ways instead of the highways and Interstates where I felt less confident.

I was almost through Ohio when I saw it in the distance. A rusted light blue water tower rose up from the ground like the clenched fist of a railroad bull. I could just make out the faded shapes of four red wooden shoes. They appeared as ghosts, for the people who had once occupied them had faded almost beyond recognition. But I could still see them: the woman with her exaggerated pigtails. The man with his one-strap overalls.

I drove on until the tower was upon me, and I veered off the road and stopped on the shoulder. I would not have recognized the area had it not been for that water tower. It was unseemly that the place where I lost Teeny was so unremarkable. But I didn't have time for silly musings, for I was instantly surrounded by the mythology of that long-ago life, so much in fact that my gut fluttered, as if a fairytale had roused me with a sharp kick.

I unfolded myself out of my rental car and made my way through the hip-high grasses toward the water tower. The rail tracks were almost hidden by the over-growth.

Before I had walked two feet, I was the scared boy again. Four feet. I was the serious teenager who protected Teeny by not smiling. Six feet. I touched the base of the tower, and I felt that manchild return as if a spirit was bent on inhabiting my body. I looked at my hands, expecting to find dirty fingernails. I glanced down and wondered why my pants weren't patched at the knee. Looking around me, I saw the ghosts of the past in a dizzying whirlwind: the hoboes running in all directions. The steam locomotive belching its chug-along song. So real was my vision that I waved to Vic, who was hanging on to a catwalk and waving at me. I turned, silly old man that I was, and held out my hand to steady Teeny, but she had already fallen. I felt the slow motion of every sluggish move, as if memories required so much energy and I had only fumes left to move me. And then, the scene, like the little girls in Teeny's stories, left me, and the vision of my old friends along with them.

Did they know, wherever they were in the world, that it was late July, the eve of our third day? Tomorrow it would be the third day after we were separated that final time. The third day, plus sixty years. Do you remember what I told you about Vic? That he insisted we always know the day and the date. I think he believed this elevated us a fraction above the poor souls who had given up and did not care if it was Tuesday or Friday. Who ceased to see a calendar in their minds.

I returned to my car and turned again onto the dusty country road and doubled back to a roadside motel I had passed earlier. I unpacked my small suitcase and washed my face in the sink. When I called my little Mia to tell her I was delayed because I was driving back, she was concerned, of course, but not overly. I had the cellular phone she had made me buy.

The oddities that I saw on the road in my youth continued to pop up here and there. That afternoon I settled into a booth in a restaurant shaped like a coffee pot. Truly. I sat at a window nearest the spout and could see the water tower. I ate a hamburger, with its waxy and limp smell, and drank a coffee that was so bad even I knew it. I did not allow myself to think that I would find Teeny the next day. I wasn't foolish enough to think that the third day, sixty years too late, would render anything but disappointment. But would it not have been equally as foolish not to try? It was not as if I had embarked on an odyssey, walking to the ends of the earth to pluck an apple from a tree that did not yet exist. It merely had been happenstance that had brought me to the intersection of time and geography. I knew happenstance could be fool's gold. But maybe I would make it shine.

I slept in my clothes that night. As I opened the suitcase to lift out my pajamas, it did not feel right. Part of me was back on the road. I had left footprints and DNA at that water tower. It would not have been right to sleep in anything but the clothes I had traveled in that day. I lay down on top of the bed, and fell into a deep sleep, for I was weary. Remember, I was in my seventies then, recently widowed, burdened with memories, and fatigued by decisions I seemed unable to resist. You have heard the phrase people sometimes use: "sleep the sleep of the dead." I wasn't quite there. I was sleeping the sleep of the unknown.

I awoke near dawn, hearing Teeny's voice, the way it drew itself out and turned a corner. Outside, the rain was tapping out its Morse Code and my subconscious had absorbed the rhythm, for I had dreamt about the little girl who had never felt rain, not even on the tip of her freckled, button nose. It was the last story I heard Teeny tell on the road.

"Can you just imagine," Teeny had asked a group of 'boes, "what it would be like to never go outside?"

A few of them shifted, but no one answered. It was a hot night in August and we were in Maine. So many blueberries had we picked that our hands and faces were stained. As we listened that evening, we handed round a pail of soapy water and a rag.

"Well, there was a little girl, tucked away in a small village in Tennessee, who did not have to imagine, for she had never been outside. Not even once. Her parents ran a general store and post office, and they kept her inside because they loved her so much.

"The couple had two baby boys before the little girl was born. The oldest boy was struck dead by a runaway horse. A few years later, the other son was stung by a wasp, and he swelled to almost double his size, so that his skin began to crack, and soon he could not breathe, and so he died, too. The next year, the couple welcomed a tiny little girl to their world. She was born at home and the couple decided that to keep her safe, they would never let her go outside.

"The little girl never knew what rain tasted like. Never felt the tickle of the sun's ray on her face. She saw all this, of course, from the window seat in her bedroom. But life is meant to be felt with all the senses. Confined as she was to the indoors, she never did understand what weather was. But rain fascinated her, for she could both see and hear it. Sometimes, lying in bed, she would count the pings of drops as they landed on the tin roof above her.

"The girl was happiest when she was having pretend tea with her dolls and teddy bear. Her parents had outfitted a beautiful room for her, with ruffled curtains and little girl furniture painted with yellow daffodils. Soon, the dolls began to talk of their lives, of how happy they were in their stiff pinafores and shoes that never had to be polished. Why, they told her, she could almost be a porcelain doll herself, so fair and smooth was her skin, for it had never been weathered by the sun, you see. The rag doll, with her red yarn hair and black stitched eyes, said that she was one hundred years old, and had belonged to the girl's great-grandmother. There was a baby doll with a plastic head and a stuffed body, but she only gurgled. The stout Queen Victoria doll, with her ancient burgundy dress and muted face, told the girl that the dolls never had to eat or drink and were never hungry or cold. They had each other for conversation. They did not have to brush their teeth or take cod liver oil. They had no parents to tell them to say their prayers, eat their vegetables, or brush their teeth.

"Slowly, as the weeks and months passed and the girl turned six years old, the voices of the dolls became louder. They could turn her into a doll, they told her, bit by bit. It would be such a slow transformation that her parents would not notice. Only when the transformation was complete, and the girl doll was sitting in a tiny chair, would the parents notice that she was gone. And they would think that she had run off and would go out into the world and look for her, not knowing that she was with them all the while.

"The girl protested. She told the dolls that she could not do that to her parents, who had already lost two children. But the dolls had already begun to change her, and once begun, the transformation could not be reversed. She began to shrink until she could barely climb into bed. She had to push over a little stool and climb upon it to reach her mattress. Before long, the girl noticed that she was no longer hungry, and didn't need to sleep. One morning, her mother came to wake her and when she began to sob and scream, the girl knew that her transformation was complete. The girl doll tried to call out to her mother, but her voice was so small, and so far away, the girl herself barely heard it. At first, she was sad. But there was nothing she could do. She took comfort in the knowledge that she would not be lonely, for she had all of her doll friends to play with. And they had promised that together they would enjoy good conversation and riddles. She waited for her mother to move her from the bed and settle her at the little table with her doll friends. When she was moved, she began to talk to the porcelain Queen Victoria doll, but the doll did not answer her. The mouth that once spoke words did not move its pink painted lips. The rag doll never blinked her black stitched eyes. The baby doll did not gurgle. It went on like this for months, then years. For you see, the voices the girl had heard were only in her head. One day, her mother moved her to the window seat and for the rest of her life, which was, of course, eternity, she watched the weather from the inside, wondering what it would feel like to touch snow or taste rain."

I smiled when I remembered that story. Yes, I know, it has a sad ending. But I smiled because I remember that afterward, as I looked around the campfire, I saw a little boy 'bo named Tully wipe his eyes and pretend that it was the smoke from the campfire that drove his tears. And then Teeny moved to sit beside him, and she wrapped her arms around him. Then she held his hand and let him cry. I had watched them, and imagined that one day, she would come to me and hold my hand. I could almost feel it resting in hers.

The dream was fading, so I rose and prepared for the day. That day, I told myself, was either the day I found Teeny, or just another day.

And what of Vic? I cannot explain why, but I knew that Vic would never do anything as sentimental as look back upon a former life and chase it down as we had once chased trains. Vic might still be in Utah. Perhaps he cut the timber he had once begged me to fell. Perhaps he had been killed on the beaches of Normandy. Truth be told, if I wanted to pay tribute to Vic, then I should stop the musings and superstitions and get on with the business at hand.

It was still too early to return to the field watched over by the water tower, so I fortified myself with sausage biscuits and orange juice at the coffee pot-shaped restaurant. I recalled the first proper restaurant breakfast the three of us ate together, where the waitress had given us free refills of coffee. I could still taste the tang of the apple cake, infused with cloves and cinnamon, which she had treated us to. Teeny had given herself a nickname that day. And Vic had given me mine.

From my lonely breakfast table, I craned my neck so I could see the top bulge of the water tower. The tall grasses whispered to me, even at my table. I put my palm to my chin, the better to think. The better to see. When I saw Teeny again, I would have to remember to ask her name. I saw the grasses lean against each other in a morning fog that had not yet lifted its dewy cloak.

149

Chapter Twenty-Three

I saw Teeny in that morning fog. Remember how small she was? In the tall grasses I could only see the top of her head as she walked across the field toward the water tower. I did not dare look away or even blink, lest the vision be just that. I willed her to turn and look at me, but I did not move my lips for fear I had conjured her.

So, we had come full circle, she and I. And suddenly we were in one of Teeny's long-ago fairytales, with an hourglass and its backward sifting sand. I did not question what was happening, for Teeny had a magic that required no wand, no spell, no explanation.

I had imagined so many times that our reunion might be much like our first on that Iowa farm when Vic and I had traveled west and returned six weeks later. Teeny had flung herself into my arms upon our return, and I had closed my eyes, the better to absorb her scent.

We were now ghosts, she and I, once so far and so long out of reach. I let the tears flow shamelessly and slip under my chin. I held out my arms and folded her into me. I breathed her in.

I was sure I heard her whisper, *Sonny Boy, oh Sonny Boy.*

Oh, how wonderful it was to hear that long-ago name trilled by her voice.

She was still so slight. Bones like a bird. Voice out of time. Skin once glass.

When I pulled away from her, my embrace shifted to our hands, and we stood there a moment. There was no need to speak yet. The words were all around us in their own story. The water tower spoke of our darkest day. The grasses whispered their approval at our reunion. The ground beneath us murmured the passing of years. I tucked her hand into the crook of my arm, like one cradles the most fragile of all things: a human life.

It all came together there: vision, memory, dreams. Perfect or imperfect. Real or not. It did not matter.

We sat in the grass and she brought out her worn drawstring bag, a tattered relic of the road.

I leaned into her and she began to speak, the dry grasses no longer rustling, for they knew I needed to hear her soft voice. Gone were her dramatic words and flourishes of plot and scene. Her tale was sparse, and tired. Like me, she had not the energy for embellishment or flair.

She told me that for ten years she had come to this place on the third day. The wretched day that never was. She waited to do this until after her husband died, just as I had started my search once my Millie was gone. There was a grace in that and we shared it, like you might share half of your sweet roll with your best friend.

"So many years have gone by," I whispered, and she held out her hand for mine.

She did not know where to start her tale.

I squeezed her hand. "When the bulls took you, did you see me? Did you hear me?"

Her eyes were closed. She shook her head no. The bull had boxed her ears so hard all she heard for days was a ringing.

She took a ragged little breath and began her story. It was the first, but would not be the last, I asked her to tell.

The bulls had sent her to a Red Cross station outside of Chicago. Because she was so small, everyone believed her when she said she was fifteen, instead of nineteen. It meant being sent to a home for girls rather than turned out onto the streets. From the orphanage, she went into a Red Cross nursing program, picking up the road again as a traveling nurse.

I imagined Teeny in the sharp white dress of the nurse who held the raffle baby in her story. I saw the red cross emblazoned on her starched nurse's cap.

"Did you ever think of us?" I asked. "Me and Vic?"

She squeezed my hand then, and I saw the tears on her face.

You were always with me, she assured me. As the end of her life neared, she needed to see me one more time. To see her sweet Sonny Boy. To see the man I had become.

My nickname hung in the air between us, and I wanted it to linger there forever.

She asked about Vic, and I told her of our brief time together without her before he moved on to the CCC. I told her about Murlona and Early, and my Millie. And of the quiet, ordered life I had made for myself.

She would have expected nothing else from me, she said.

I had only a small time with Teeny in my life, nearer to the beginning and once again, nearer the end. But that somehow was enough. And the middle had been for my Millie. And that would never change.

I asked Teeny for one last story and pulled the copy of the newspaper article from my wallet. Years earlier I had trimmed it down, and it was now creased and greasy from the folding and re-folding. I told her the story of how I had come across the article so many years ago, and how the years had jumbled to deceive me, for she was too old to be that baby.

I put the paper in her shaking hand. She clutched it to her chest as if she might nurse a babe.

And then I saw the truth of it all.

She was not the baby.

She was the mother.

And so, this was her secret. An unseen thing that was everywhere we went, the three of us, in the Big Trouble. She had buried an unspoken tragedy under fantasy. I now saw the fairytales she told for what they really were. They were not stories for us. They were for her, because make-believe was easier than reality. Teeny used her stories to stop an unknown ending. An unknown ending is the vast ceaselessness of the universe, and impossible to reach. A new ending is the cork in a leaking bucket. A reprieve from damage.

I saw her daughter then. The gypsy girl swirling and laughing, silver bracelets clinking, orange velvet shoes dancing for their supper. And then the novice with rebellious red curls springing forth as she freed them from her nun's habit. The little girl folding paper into a family. The orphan in the white dress and buttercup sash who died from happiness.

The raffle baby had been with us all along, an unknowable apparition who cast an invisible shadow wherever we went.

"And the father?" I asked gently.

Teeny turned her face and I watched a tear trail down her cheek. Instantly I knew I had broken the pledge of the hoboes: never ask where they come from—only where they are going.

Presently she opened the drawstring bag and from it withdrew a small silver compact. Something inside me stirred.

She smiled and asked if I remembered when she found it.

I nodded, the solemn gesture of a pharaoh.

She opened the compact and showed me the cracked mirror. Our eyes met in the tiny glass, as if ours had been a separation of millimeters rather than decades. She asked that I rouge her cheeks, which I did, but only as well as an old man could. She motioned again to the bag and I rummaged inside until I came upon another familiar object. I placed the small bottle of red nail polish in her hand, but she shook her head and held her hand out to me.

I shook the bottle, as I had seen my little Mia do, and drew out the brush. My large, gnarled hands were clumsy for such delicate work. Nevertheless, I applied the polish, slowly and meticulously. Then she asked me to do her hair and I pulled a comb from the bag. I brushed the cascade that whispered around her shoulders. I separated the strands into a trinity of silver ropes. I knew the Father, Son, and Holy Ghost would arrive soon to spirit her away.

There were so many things I still wanted to know. Why would she not replace the boots that were her downfall? What became of the baby? What was her name?

You are wondering these things, too. You. My faithful friend. Our journey together is also coming to an end. I will miss our time together. I hope you will, too.

There was no time for questions. I felt the breeze that would spirit her away from me again. I would have to wait until eternity to hear the answers. But I got my wish, did I not? To say good-bye. To write the end of the story. How many of us have a life-long wish granted in the time it takes an eyelash to rest upon the cheek? How many of us can create the end of our own fairytale?

And so, I plaited her hair. When I tied it off with a yellow ribbon, I rested the braid on her shoulder, and she kissed my hand and pressed it to her cheek.

- The End -

If you enjoyed *The Raffle Baby* please leave a rating/review and follow me on Goodreads and BookBub. Sign up for news at ruth talbot.com. Thank you.

Acknowledgments

Nothing is possible without the love and encouragement of my husband.

Many thanks to my sister for her constant love and support.

And thank you to Murlona Austrum for the loan of her beautiful name.

About the Author

Ruth Talbot is a fiction writer in Minneapolis, Minnesota, where she lives with her husband and rescue pup. She loves to comb through old newspapers online and this is how she found the story of the raffle baby.

Contact Ruth and sign up for news at ruthtalbot.com.

 facebook.com/RuthTalbotAuthor

 bookbub.com/authors/ruth-talbot

 tiktok.com/@ruth_talbot_author

ISBN 979-8-40680121-5

Made in the USA
Monee, IL
15 November 2022

17794860R00097